PRAISE FOR *FEVER DREAM*

**SHORTLISTED FOR THE
MAN BOOKER INTERNATIONAL PRIZE**

**SELECTED AS A BOOK OF THE YEAR BY
THE *OBSERVER, FINANCIAL TIMES, GUARDIAN*
& *EVENING STANDARD***

'A book to read in one sitting – bold, uncanny and utterly gripping.'   *Observer*, Best Fiction of the Year

'A nauseous, eerie read, sickeningly good.'
Emma Cline, bestselling author of *The Girls*

'Transcends the sensational plot elements to achieve a powerful and humane vision.'
Financial Times, Best Books of the Year

'A gloriously creepy fable.'
Guardian, Best Fiction of the Year

'A spare, hypnotic literary page-turner.'
O, the Oprah Magazine

'Dazzling, unforgettable, and deeply strange. I've never read anything like it.'
Evening Standard, Books of the Year

'Mesmerizing.'   *Washington Post*

'Subtle, dreamy and indelibly creepy.'
Economist, Best Books of the Year

'Read this in a single sitting and by the end I could hardly breathe. It's a total mind-wrecker. Amazing. Thrilling.'   Max Porter, author of *Lanny*

'Punches far above its weight... The sort of book that makes you look under the bed last thing at night and sleep with the light on.'   *Daily Mail*

'The genius of *Fever Dream* is less in what it says than in how Schweblin says it, with a design at once so enigmatic and so disciplined that the book feels as if it belongs to a new literary genre altogether.'
                    The New Yorker

PRAISE FOR *LITTLE EYES*

LONGLISTED FOR THE INTERNATIONAL BOOKER PRIZE

A *GUARDIAN* & *TIMES* BEST NOVEL OF THE YEAR A *SUNDAY TIMES* BEST SCIENCE FICTION BOOK OF THE YEAR * AN NPR BEST BOOK OF THE YEAR

'Ingenious... An artful exploration of solitude and empathy in a globalised world... In a nimble, fast-moving narrative, what's most impressive is the way she foregrounds her characters' inner hopes and fears.'
                    Guardian

'This has a propulsive, Dave Eggers-ish readability.'
                    Daily Mail

'Disturbing... Schweblin enjoys hovering just above the normal. Inspired by Samuel Beckett, she is interested in exposing absurdities.' *Financial Times*

'*Little Eyes* makes for masterfully uneasy reading; it's a book that burrows under your skin.'
Daily Telegraph

'Wonderfully chilly, astute and borderline-horrific.'
The Sunday Times, Best Sci-fi Books of the Year

'I cannot remember a book so efficient in establishing character and propelling narrative; there's material for a hundred novels in these deft, rich 242 pages... The writing, ably translated from the Spanish by Megan McDowell, is superb, fully living up to the promise of Schweblin's stunning previous novel, *Fever Dream*... A slim volume as expansive and ambitious as an epic.'
New York Times

'In Samanta Schweblin's fiendishly readable *Little Eyes* the new must-have tech gadget allows users to leapfrog into the lives of strangers – a sharp idea that became even more pertinent with the isolation and atomisation of lockdown.' *Guardian*, Best Fiction of the Year

'A timely meditation on humanity and technology.'
Harper's Bazaar

'*Little Eyes* acts as a clear warning that every digital decision we make has consequences... It does feel alarmingly real.' *i*

Also by Samanta Schweblin

Fever Dream

Mouthful of Birds

Little Eyes

Seven

Empty

Houses

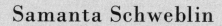

Samanta Schweblin

Translated by Megan McDowell

ONEWORLD

A Oneworld Book

First published in the United Kingdom, the Republic of Ireland and Australia
by Oneworld Publications, 2022
First published in Spain as *Siete casas vacías* by
Editorial Páginas de Espuma, Madrid, 2015

Published by arrangement with Riverhead Books,
an imprint of Penguin Publishing Group, a division of
Penguin Random House LLC

ISBN 978-0-86154-432-5
eISBN 978-0-86154-433-2

Book design by Meighan Cavanaugh
Printed and bound in Great Britain by Clays Ltd, Elcograf S.p.A.

Grateful acknowledgment is made for permission from the family of
Juan Luis Martínez to print an excerpt in translation from his poem
'La desaparición de una familia' from *La nueva novela*.

Oneworld Publications
10 Bloomsbury Street
London WC1B 3SR
England

To Liliana and Pablo,

my parents

Before his five-year-old daughter
got lost between the dining room and the kitchen,
he had warned her: "This house is neither large nor small,
but make the least mistake and the road signs will disappear,
and of this lifetime at last, you will have lost all hope."

—~~Juan Luis Martínez~~, "The Disappearance of a Family"

A: I like your apartment.

B: It's nice, but it's only big enough for one person—or
two people who are very close.

A: You know two people who are very close?

—Andy Warhol, *The Philosophy of Andy Warhol*

CONTENTS

Seven Empty Houses

None

of

That

W e're lost," says my mother.

She brakes and leans over the steering wheel. Her fingers, slender and old, grip the plastic tightly. We're over half an hour from home, in one of the residential neighborhoods we like the most. There are beautiful and spacious mansions here, but the roads are unpaved, and they're muddy because it rained all last night.

"Did you have to stop right in the mud? How are we going to get out of here now?"

I open my door to see how deep the wheels are stuck. Pretty deep, deep enough. I slam my door.

"Just what is it you're doing, Mom?"

"What do you mean, what am I doing?" Her confusion seems genuine.

I know exactly what it is we're doing, but I've only just realized how strange it is. My mother doesn't seem to understand, but she does respond, so she must know what I'm referring to.

"We're looking at houses," she says.

She blinks a couple of times; she has too much mascara on her eyelashes.

"Looking at houses?"

"Looking at houses." She indicates the houses on either side of us.

They are immense. They gleam atop their hills of freshly mown lawns, shining in the dazzling light of the setting sun. My mother sighs, and without letting go of the wheel she leans back in the seat. She's not going to say much more. Maybe she doesn't know what else to say. But that is exactly what we do. Go out to look at houses. We go out to look at other people's houses. Any attempt to figure out why could turn into the straw that breaks the camel's back, confirmation of the fact that my mother has been throwing her own daughter's time into the garbage for as long as I can remember. My mother shifts into first gear, and to my surprise the wheels spin for a moment but she manages to move the car forward. I look back at the intersection, the mess we made of the sandy dirt of the road, and I pray that no caretaker catches on that we did the same thing yesterday, two intersections down, and then again when we were nearly at the exit. We keep moving. My mother drives straight, without stopping in front of any of the mansions. She doesn't comment on the huge windows or fancy doors, the hammocks or awnings. She doesn't sigh or hum any song. She doesn't jot down addresses. Doesn't look at me. A few blocks down, the houses grow more spaced out and the grassy lawns flatten: carefully trimmed by gardeners and with no sidewalks in the way, they start right there at the dirt road and spread over the perfectly leveled terrain, like a mirror of green water flush with the earth. She takes a left and drives a little farther. She says aloud, but to herself:

"There's no way out of this."

There are some houses farther on, and then a forest closes in on the road.

"There's a lot of mud," I say. "Turn around without stopping the car."

She looks at me with a frown, then pulls close to the grass on the right and tries to turn back the other way. The result is terrible: just as she manages to get the car in a vaguely diagonal position, she runs up against the grass on the left, and brakes.

"Shit," she says.

She accelerates, and the wheels spin in the mud. I look back to study the scene. There's a boy outside, almost on the threshold of the house behind us. My mother shifts gears, accelerates again, and manages to move in reverse. And this is what she does now: with the car in reverse, she drives across the street, goes into the yard in front of the boy's house, and draws, from one side to the other across the wide blanket of freshly cut grass, a double-lined semicircle of mud. The car stops in front of the house's picture window. The boy is standing there holding his plastic truck, transfixed. I raise my hand in a gesture that wants to apologize, or warn, but he drops the truck and runs into the house. My mother looks at me.

"Go," I say.

The wheels spin and the car doesn't move.

"Slowly, Mom!"

A woman pushes aside the window curtains and looks out at us, at her yard. The boy is next to her, pointing. The curtain closes again, and my mother sinks the car deeper and deeper. The woman comes out of the house and starts to walk over to us, but she doesn't want to trample her grass. She takes the first steps along the path of varnished wood, then corrects course to come toward us, practically walking on tiptoe. My mother says *shit* again, under her breath. She lets off the accelerator, and also, finally, lets go of the steering wheel.

The woman reaches us and leans over to talk to us through the car window. She wants to know what we are doing in her yard, and she doesn't ask nicely. The boy looks on, hugging one of the columns by the entrance. My mother says she's sorry, she's really very sorry, and she says it several times. But the woman doesn't seem to hear. She just looks at her yard, at the wheels sunk into

7

the lawn, and she repeats her question about what we're doing there, why we are stuck in her yard, if we understand the damage we've just done. So I explain it to her. I say that my mother doesn't know how to drive in the mud. That my mother is not well. And then my mother bangs her forehead into the steering wheel and stays like that, dead or paralyzed, who knows. Her back shudders and she starts to cry. The woman looks at me. She doesn't know what to do. I shake my mother. Her forehead doesn't move from the steering wheel, and her arms fall dead to her sides. I get out of the car, apologize to the woman again. She is tall and blond, brawny like the boy, and her eyes, nose, and mouth are too close together for the size of her head. She looks the same age as my mother.

"Who is going to pay for this?" she asks.

I don't have any money, but I tell her we'll pay for it. That I'm sorry and, of course, we will pay. That seems to calm her down. She turns her attention back to my mother for a moment, without forgetting about her yard.

"Ma'am, are you feeling okay? What were you trying to do?"

My mother raises her head and looks at the woman. "I feel terrible. Call an ambulance, please."

The woman doesn't seem to know whether my mother is being serious or pulling her leg. Of course she is serious, even if the ambulance isn't necessary. I shake my head at the woman to say she should wait and not make any calls. The woman takes a few steps back, looks at my mother's old, rusty car, and then at her astonished son behind her. She doesn't want us to be here, she wants us to disappear, but she doesn't know how to make that happen.

"Please," says my mother, "could you bring me a glass of water before the ambulance gets here?"

The woman is slow to move; she seems not to want to leave us alone in her yard.

"Okay," she says.

She walks away, grabs the boy by the shirt, and pulls him inside with her. The front door slams shut.

"Could you please tell me what you're doing, Mom? Get out of the car, I'm going to try to move it."

My mother sits up straight in the seat, moves her legs slowly as she starts to get out. I look around for medium-sized logs or some rocks to use as ramps for the wheels, but everything is so neat and tidy. There's nothing but lawn and flowers.

"I'm going to look for some wood," I tell my mother, pointing toward the forest at the end of the street. "Don't move."

My mother, who was in the process of getting out of the car, freezes a moment and then drops back into her seat. I'm worried because night is falling, and I don't know if I'll be able to get the car out in the dark. The forest is only two houses away. I walk into the trees, and it takes a few minutes to find exactly what I need. When I get back, my mother is not in the car. There's no one outside. I approach the front door of the house. The boy's truck is lying on the doormat. I ring the doorbell and the woman comes to open the door.

"I called the ambulance," she says. "I didn't know where you were, and your mother said she was going to faint again."

I wonder when the first time was. I walk in carrying the pieces of wood. I have two, the size of two bricks. The woman leads me to the kitchen. We walk through two spacious, carpeted living rooms, and then I hear my mother's voice.

"Is this white marble? How do they get white marble? What does your daddy do, sweetheart?"

She's sitting at the table, a mug in one hand and the sugar bowl in the other. The boy is sitting across from her, looking at her.

"Let's go," I tell her, showing her the wood.

"Look at the design of this sugar bowl," says my mother, pushing it toward me. But when she sees I'm unimpressed, she adds, "I really do feel very bad."

"That one's for decoration," says the boy. "This is our real sugar bowl."

He pushes a different, wooden sugar bowl toward my mother. She ignores him, stands up, and, as if she were about to vomit, leaves the kitchen. I follow her resignedly. She locks herself in a small bathroom off the hallway. The woman and her son look at me but don't follow. I knock on the door, ask if I can come in, and wait. The woman peers at us from the kitchen.

"They say the ambulance will be here in fifteen minutes."

"Thanks," I say.

The bathroom door opens. I go in and close it behind me. I put the wood down beside the mirror. My mother is crying, sitting on the toilet lid.

"What's wrong, Mom?"

Before answering she folds a bit of toilet paper and blows her nose.

"Where do people get all these things? And did you see there's a staircase on either side of the living room?" She rests her face in the palms of her hands. "It makes me so sad I just want to die."

There's a knock at the door and I remember the ambulance is on its way. The woman asks if we're all right. I have to get my mother out of this house.

"I'm going to get the car out," I say, picking the wood up again. "I want you out there with me in two minutes. You'd better be there."

The woman is in the hall talking on a cell phone, but she sees me and hangs up.

"It's my husband, he's on his way."

I wait for an expression that will tell me whether the man is coming to help my mother and me, or to help the woman get us out of the house. But the woman just stares at me, taking care not to give me any clues. I go outside and walk to the car, and I can hear the boy running behind me. I don't say anything as I prop the wood under the wheels and look around to see where my mother could have left the keys. Then I start the car. It takes several tries, but finally the ramp trick works. I close the car door, and the boy has to run so I don't hit him. I don't stop, I retrace the semicircular tracks back to the road. She's not going to come out on her own, I tell myself. Why would she listen to me and come out of the house like a normal mother? I turn off the car and go inside to get her. The boy runs behind me, hugging the muddy pieces of wood.

I enter without knocking and head straight for the bathroom.

"She's not in the bathroom anymore," says the woman. "Please, get your mother out of the house. This has gone too far."

She leads me to the second floor. The staircase is spacious and light, and a cream-colored rug marks the way. The woman goes up first, blind to the muddy footprints

I leave on each step. She points to a room with the door half open, and I go in without opening it all the way, in order to maintain a semblance of privacy. My mother is lying facedown on the carpet in the middle of the master bedroom. The sugar bowl is on the dresser, along with her watch and bracelets, which for some reason she has taken off. Her arms and legs are splayed wide, and for a moment I wonder if there is any other way to hug a thing as massive as a house, and if that is in fact what my mother is trying to do. She sighs and then sits up on the floor, smooths her shirt and her hair, looks at me. Her face is less red now, but the tears have made a mess of her makeup.

"What's going on now?" she asks.

"The car's ready. We're leaving."

I peer outside to get a sense of what the woman is doing, but I don't see her.

"And what are we going to do with all of this?" asks my mother, gesturing around herself. "Someone has to talk to these people."

"Where's your purse?"

"Downstairs, in the living room. The first living

room, because there's a bigger one that looks out onto the pool, and another one past the kitchen, facing the backyard. There are three living rooms." My mother takes a tissue from her jeans pocket, blows her nose, and dries her tears. "Each one for something different."

She gets up holding on to a bedpost and walks toward the en suite bathroom.

The bed is made with a fold in the top sheet that I've only ever seen my mother make. Under the bed are a balled-up bedspread with fuchsia and yellow stars and a dozen small throw pillows.

"Mom, my god, did you make the bed?"

"Don't even get me started on those pillowcases," she says, and then, peering out from behind the door to be sure I hear: "And I want to see that sugar bowl when I come out of the bathroom. Don't you do anything crazy."

"What sugar bowl?" asks the woman from the other side of the bedroom door. She knocks three times but doesn't dare enter. "My sugar bowl? Please, it was my mother's."

From the bathroom comes the sound of water running in the tub. My mother goes over to the bedroom door and for a second I think she's going to let the woman in, but instead she closes it and starts gesturing at me to keep my voice down, that the faucet is running so no one can hear us. This is my mother, I tell myself, while she opens the dresser drawers and pushes aside the clothes to inspect the bottoms, making sure the wood inside is also cedar. For as long as I can remember, we've gone out to look at houses, removed unsuitable flowers and pots from their gardens. We've moved sprinklers, straightened mailboxes, relocated lawn ornaments that were too heavy for the grass. As soon as my feet reached the pedals, I started to take over driving, which gave my mother more freedom. Once, by herself, she moved a white wooden bench and put it in the yard of the house across the street. She unhooked hammocks. Yanked up malignant weeds. Three times she pulled off the name "Marilú 2" from a terribly cheesy sign. My father found out about one or another of these events, but I don't think that was why he left my mother. When he went, my father took all his things except the car key, which he left on one of the piles of my mother's home and garden magazines, and for some years after that she almost never got out of the car on any of our excursions. She'd sit in the passenger seat and say "That's *kikuyu*," "That *bow window* is not American," "The *cascading geranium* flowers should not be beside the *spotted lady's thumb*," "If I ever decide to paint the house that shade of *pearl pink*, please, hire someone to just shoot me." But it was a long time before she got out of the car again. Today, however, she has crossed a big line. She insisted on driving. She contrived to get us inside this house, into the master bedroom, and now she's just come back from the bathroom after dumping two jars of salts into the tub, and she's starting to throw some products from the dressing table into the trash. I hear a car pull up, and I peek out the window that overlooks the backyard. It's almost night now, but I see them. He's getting out of the car and the woman is already walking toward him. Her left hand is holding the little boy's, her right hand working double-time making gestures and signals. He nods in alarm, looks toward the second floor. He sees me, and when he sees me, I realize that we have to move fast.

"We're leaving, Mom."

She's removing the hooks from the shower curtain, but I take them from her hand and throw them to the floor, grab her by the wrist, and push her toward the stairs. It's pretty violent; I have never treated my mother like this. A new fury drives me toward the door. My mother follows, tripping on the stairs. The pieces of wood are at the foot of the steps and I kick them as I pass. We reach the living room, I pick up my mother's purse, and we go out the front door.

Once we're in the car, as we're reaching the corner, I think I see the lights of another car pulling out of the house's driveway and turning in our direction, following us. I reach the first muddy intersection at full speed as my mother says:

"What kind of madness was all that?"

I wonder if she's referring to my part or hers. In a gesture of protest, my mother buckles her seat belt. Her purse is on her lap and her fists close tight around its handles. I tell myself, *Now, you calm down, you calm down, you calm down.* I check the rearview mirror for the other car but don't see anyone. I want to talk to my mother, but I can't help yelling at her.

"What are you looking for, Mom? What is all of this?"

She doesn't even move. She stares straight ahead, serious, her forehead terribly furrowed.

"Please, Mom, what is it? What the hell are we doing at other people's houses?"

An ambulance siren wails in the distance.

"Do you want one of those living rooms? Is that what you want? Those marble countertops? The damned sugar bowl? Those useless kids? Is that it? What the fuck are you missing from those houses?"

I pound the steering wheel. The ambulance siren sounds closer and I dig my nails into the plastic. Once, when I was five years old and my mother cut all the calla lilies from a garden, she forgot me and left me sitting against the fence, and she didn't have the guts to come back for me. I waited a long time, until I heard the shouts of a German woman who came out of the house brandishing a broom, and I ran. My mother was circling the house in a two-block radius, and it took us a long time to find each other.

"None of that," says my mother, keeping her gaze

forward, and that's the last thing she says during the whole drive.

A few blocks ahead, the ambulance turns toward us and then hurtles past.

We get home half an hour later. We drop our things on the table and kick off our muddy sneakers. The house is cold, and from the kitchen I watch my mother skirt the sofa, go into the bedroom, sit down on her bed, and reach over to turn on the radiator. I put the kettle on for tea. This is what I need right now, I tell myself, a little tea, and I sit beside the stove to wait. As I'm putting the tea bag into the mug, the doorbell rings. It's the woman, the owner of the house with three living rooms. I open the door and stand looking at her. I ask how she knows where we live.

"I followed you," she says, looking down at her shoes.

She has a different attitude now, more fragile and patient, and though I open the screen door to let her in, she can't seem to bring herself to take the first step. I look both ways down the street, but I don't see any car a woman like her could have driven here.

"I don't have the money," I say.

"No," she says, "don't worry, I didn't come for that. I . . . is your mother here?"

I hear the bedroom door close. It's a loud slam, but maybe it's hard to hear from outside.

I shake my head. She looks down at her shoes again and waits.

"Can I come in?"

I point her to a chair at the table. On the brick-tiled floor, her heels make a noise different from our heels, and I see her move carefully: the spaces of this house are more cramped, and the woman doesn't seem to feel at ease. She leaves her bag on her crossed legs.

"Would you like some tea?"

She nods.

"Your mother . . ." she says.

I hand her a hot mug and I think, *Your mother is in my house again. Your mother wants to know how I pay for the leather upholstery on all my sofas.*

"Your mother took my sugar bowl," says the woman.

She smiles almost apologetically, stirs her tea, looks at it, but doesn't drink it.

"It seems silly," she says, "but of all the things in the house, that's all I have left of my mother, and . . ." She makes a strange sound, almost like a hiccup, and her eyes fill with tears. "I need that sugar bowl. You have to give it back."

We sit a moment in silence. She avoids my eyes. I glance out at the backyard and I see her, I see my mother, and then I distract the woman to keep her from looking out there, too.

"You want your sugar bowl?" I ask.

"Is it here?" asks the woman, and she immediately stands up, looks at the kitchen counter, the living room, the bedroom door nearby.

But I can't stop thinking about what I've just seen: my mother kneeling on the ground under the clothes hanging on the line, putting the sugar bowl into a fresh hole in the earth.

"If you want it, find it yourself," I say.

The woman stares at me, takes several seconds to absorb what I've just said. Then she sets her purse on the table and walks slowly away. She seems to have trouble moving between the couch and the TV, between all the towers of stackable boxes, as if no place were good enough to start her search. That's how I realize what it is that I want. I want her to look. I want her to move our things. I want her to inspect, set aside, and take apart. To remove everything from the boxes, to trample, re-arrange, to throw herself on the ground, and also to cry. And I want my mother to come inside. Because if my mother comes in here right now, if she composes herself quickly after her newest burial and comes back to the kitchen, she'll be relieved to see how this is done by a woman who doesn't have her years of experience, or a house where she can do these kinds of things well, the way they should be done.

My Parents

and

My Children

Where are your parents' clothes?" asks Marga.

She crosses her arms and waits for my answer. She knows I don't know. On the other side of the picture window, my parents are running naked in the backyard.

"It's almost six, Javier," Marga tells me. "What's going to happen when Charly comes back from the store with the kids and they see their grandparents chasing each other around?"

"Who's Charly?" I ask.

I think I know who Charly is—he's the great-new-man

my ex-wife is dating—but at some point I would like for her to explain that to me.

"They're going to die of shame when they see their grandparents, that's what's going to happen."

"They're sick, Marga."

She sighs. I take deep breaths and count slowly to keep from turning bitter, to instill patience, to give Marga the time she needs. I say:

"You wanted the kids to see their grandparents. You wanted me to bring my parents out here, because you thought this place, three hundred kilometers from my house, would be a good spot for a vacation."

"You said they were better."

Behind Marga, my father sprays my mother with the hose. When he sprays her tits, my mother holds her tits. When he sprays her ass, my mother holds her ass.

"You know how they get if you take them out of their environment," I say. "And outdoors . . ."

Is it my mother who holds what my father sprays, or is it my father who sprays what my mother holds?

"Uh-huh. So if I'm going to invite you to spend a few days with your children, whom, I might add, you haven't seen in three months, I have to anticipate the level of your parents' excitement."

My mother picks up Marga's poodle and holds it over her head, spinning around. I try to keep my eyes trained on Marga to prevent her, at all costs, from turning toward them.

"I want to leave all this madness behind, Javier."

This madness, I think.

"If that means you see the kids less.. . . I can't keep exposing them to this."

"They're just naked, Marga."

She walks forward, and I follow. Behind us, the poodle is still spinning in the air. Before opening the front door Marga checks her hair in the windowpane and adjusts her dress. Charly is tall, strong, and brutish. He looks like the guy who announces the twelve o'clock news, only his body is swollen from exercise. My four-year-old daughter and my six-year-old son hang from his arms like two swim floaties. Charly delicately helps them fall, lowering his immense gorilla torso toward the ground and freeing himself to give Marga a kiss. Then he comes toward me, and for a moment I'm afraid he won't be friendly. But he holds out his hand and he smiles.

"Javier, this is Charly," says Marga.

I feel the kids crash into my legs and hug me. I squeeze Charly's hand forcefully as he shakes my whole body. The kids pull away and run off.

"What do you think of the house, Javi?" asks Charly, his eyes looking upward and beyond me, as if it were a real and true castle they'd rented.

Javi, I think. *This madness*, I think.

The poodle appears, whimpering softly with its tail between its legs. Marga picks it up, and while the dog licks her she wrinkles her nose and coos, "My-widdle-puppums-my-widdle-puppums." Charly looks at her with his head cocked to one side, maybe just trying to understand. Then Marga turns abruptly toward him, alarmed, and says:

"Where are the kids?"

"They must be in the back," says Charly, "in the yard."

"I don't want them to see their grandparents like that."

All three of us turn from side to side, but we don't see them.

"See, Javier, this is precisely the kind of thing I want to avoid," says Marga, taking a few steps away. "Kids!"

She heads around the house toward the backyard. Charly and I follow.

"How was the road?" asks Charly.

He mimes the movement of turning a steering wheel with one hand, simulates changing gears to accelerate with the other. There is stupidity and eagerness in each one of his movements.

"I don't drive."

He bends down to pick up some toys on the path and sets them aside; now his brow is furrowed. I'm afraid of reaching the yard and finding my kids and my parents together. No, what I'm afraid of is Marga finding them together, and the great scene of recrimination that will follow. But Marga is alone in the middle of the yard, waiting for us with her fists on her hips. She heads back inside and we go into the house behind her. We are her most humble followers, and that means I have something in common with Charly, some kind of kinship. Could he really have enjoyed the highway on his drive?

"Kids!" Marga shouts up the stairs. She's furious but she contains herself, maybe because Charly still doesn't know her very well. She comes back and sits on a stool in the kitchen. "We need something to drink, don't we?"

Charly takes a bottle of soda from the refrigerator and pours three glasses. Marga takes a couple sips and sits looking out into the yard for a moment.

"This is really bad." She stands up again. "This is really bad. I mean, they could be doing anything." And now she does look at me.

"Let's check again," I say, but by then she's already headed out to the backyard.

She comes back a few seconds later.

"They're not there," she says. "My god, Javier, they're not there."

"They *are* there, Marga, they have to be somewhere."

Charly goes out the front door, crosses the front yard, and follows the dirt tracks that lead to the road. Marga goes up the stairs and calls to the kids from the second floor. I go outside and circle the house. I pass the open garage full of toys, buckets, and plastic shovels. I look up into the trees and see that the kids' inflatable dolphin has been hung, strangled, from one of the branches. The rope is made of my parents' jogging suits. Marga peers out from one of the windows and our eyes meet for a second. Is she looking for my parents, too, or just for the kids? I go into the house through the kitchen door. Charly is coming in just then through the front door, and he tells me from the living room:

"They're not in front."

His face is no longer friendly. Now he has two lines between his eyebrows and he's overdoing his movements as if Marga were controlling him: he goes quickly from stillness to action, crouching under the table, looking behind the china cabinet, peering under the stairs, as if he would be able to locate the kids only if he took them by surprise. I find myself unable to look away from his movements, and I can't focus on my own search.

"They're not outside," says Marga. "Could they have gone back to the car? The car, Charly, the car."

I wait, but there are no instructions for me. Charly goes back outside, and Marga climbs the stairs again to the bedrooms. I follow her. She enters the one that's apparently Simon's, so I check Lina's. We change rooms and look again. When I'm peering under Simon's bed, I hear her curse.

"Motherfuckers," she says, so I assume it's not because she's found the kids. Could she have found my parents?

We check the bathroom together, then the attic and the master bedroom. Marga opens the closets, pushes aside some clothes on hangers. There aren't many things and they're all very organized. It's a summer house, I tell myself, but then I think about the real house where my wife and kids live, the house that used to be mine as well, and I realize it was always that way in this family—few things, well organized—and it had never done any good to push aside the clothes in search of something else. We hear Charly come back inside, and we meet him in the living room.

"They're not in the car," he tells my wife.

"This is your parents' fault," says Marga.

She pushes me by the shoulder.

"It's your fault. Where the hell are my kids?" she shouts, and she goes running back out into the yard.

She calls to them from one side of the house and the other.

"What's beyond the shrubs?" I ask Charly.

He looks at me and then back at my wife, who is still shouting.

"Simon! Lina!"

"Are there neighbors on the other side of the bushes?" I ask.

"I don't think so. I don't know. There are estates. Parcels. The houses are really big."

He might be right to hesitate, but he seems like the stupidest man I've met in my life. Marga returns.

"I'm going first," she says, and she pushes between us. "Simon!"

"Dad!" I shout, walking behind Marga. "Mom!"

Marga is a few meters ahead of me when she stops

and picks something up from the ground. It's something blue, and she holds it with her fingertips, as if it were a dead animal. It's Lina's sweatshirt. She turns around to look at me. She's about to say something, curse me up and down again, but then she sees that farther on there's another piece of clothing and she goes toward it. I feel the looming shadow of Charly behind me. Marga picks up Lina's fuchsia shirt, and farther on one of her sneakers, and farther still, Simon's T-shirt.

There are more clothes on the road, but Marga stops short and turns back to us.

"Call the police, Charly. Call the police *now*."

"Sweetie, there's no need for that . . ." says Charly.

Sweetie, I think.

"Call the police, Charly."

Charly turns around and hurries back toward the house. Marga picks up more clothing. I follow her. She picks up another piece and stops before the last one. It's Simon's little shorts. They're yellow and a bit twisted up. Marga does nothing. Maybe she can't bend down for the shorts, maybe she doesn't have the strength. She has her back to me and her body seems to start to shake.

I approach slowly, trying not to startle her. The shorts are tiny. They could fit on my hands, four fingers in one hole, my thumb in the other.

"They'll be here in a minute," says Charly, coming out of the house. "They're sending a patrol car."

"You and your family, I'm going to . . ." says Marga, coming toward me.

"Marga . . ."

I pick up the trunks and then Marga lunges at me. I try to stand firm, but I lose my balance. I shield my face from her slaps. Charly is already here and trying to separate us. The patrol car pulls up and sounds its siren once. Two policemen get quickly out and rush to help Charly.

"My kids aren't here," says Marga, "my kids aren't here," and she points to the shorts dangling from my hand.

"Who is this man?" asks one of the cops. "Are you the husband?" they ask Charly.

We try to explain ourselves. Contrary to my first impression, neither Marga nor Charly seems to blame me. They just plead for the kids.

"My children are lost and they're with two crazy people," says Marga.

But the cops only want to know why we were fighting. Charly's chest starts to swell, and for a moment I'm afraid he's going to go after the cops. I let my hands fall in resignation the way Marga had done with me earlier, but the second cop's eyes just follow the movement of the shorts in alarm.

"What are you looking at?" asks Charly.

"What?" says the cop.

"You've been looking at those shorts since you got out of the car. You want to let someone know there are two missing kids?"

"My kids," repeats Marga. She stands firmly in front of one of the policemen and repeats it many times; she wants the cop to focus on what's important. "My kids, my kids, my kids."

"When did you see them last?" the other cop finally asks.

"They're not in the house," says Marga. "They took them."

"Who took them, ma'am?"

My Parents and My Children

I shake my head and try to interrupt, but the police beat me to it.

"Are you talking about a kidnapping?"

"They could be with their grandparents," I say.

"They're with two naked old people," says Marga.

"And whose clothing is that, ma'am?"

"It's my kids'."

"Are you telling me that there are children and adults naked and together?"

"Please," says Marga's now-broken voice.

For the first time I wonder how dangerous it really is for your kids to be going around naked with your parents.

"They could be hiding," I say. "We can't rule that out yet."

"And who are you?" asks one cop, while the other is already radioing the station.

"I'm the husband," I say.

So the officer looks at Charly now. Marga faces him down again, and I'm afraid she's going to refute my words, but she says:

"Please: my children, my children."

The first cop leaves the radio and comes over:

"Parents in the car, and the gentleman"—indicating Charly—"stays here in case the kids come back to the house."

We stand looking at him.

"Get in, let's go, we have to move fast."

"No way," says Marga.

"Ma'am, please, we have to be sure they're not going toward the highway."

Charly pushes Marga toward the patrol car and I follow her. We get in and I close my door with the car already moving. Charly is standing, looking at us, and I wonder if those three hundred kilometers of exciting driving had been done with my kids in the car. The cruiser backs up a little and we pull away and head toward the highway, fast. Just then I turn around to look at the house. I see them, all four of them: behind Charly, past the front yard, my parents and my children, naked and soaking wet in the living room's picture window. My mother is rubbing her tits against the glass and Lina does it, too, staring at her in fascination. Simon imitates the two of them with his ass cheeks. They're shouting

with joy, but no one hears. Someone yanks the shorts
from my hand and I hear Marga curse the cops. There is
noise from the radio. The police are shouting to the station, and they say the words "adults and minors" twice,
"kidnapping" once, and "naked" three times, while my
ex-wife punches her fists into the back of the driver's
seat. So I tell myself, *Don't open your mouth*, and *Not
a peep*, because I see my father looking at me: his old
torso tanned by the sun, his soft sex between his legs.
He's smiling triumphantly and he seems to recognize me.
He hugs my mother and my children, slowly, warmly,
without pulling anyone away from the glass.

It Happens

All the Time

in This House

Mr. Weimer is knocking at the door of my house. I recognize the sound of his heavy fist, his cautious, repetitive raps. So I leave the dishes in the sink and look out into the yard: there they are again, all those clothes scattered over the grass. I think about how things always happen in the same order, even the most extraordinary things, and I think it as if out loud, in an orderly way that requires a search for each word. These kinds of reflections come to me when I'm washing the dishes; all I have to do is turn on the faucet for the disjointed ideas to finally fall into place. It's just a flash of illumination, and if I turn off the water to really take note, the words disappear. Mr. Weimer's fists knock again, harder now, but he isn't a violent man; he's a poor neighbor whose wife torments him, a man who doesn't know how to go on with his life but doesn't let that keep him from trying. A man who, when he lost his son and I went to the wake to give my condolences, gave me a stiff, cold hug, and spent a few minutes talking with other guests before coming back and whispering into my ear, "I've just found out which kids are always knocking over the garbage cans. We won't have to worry about that anymore." That kind of man. When his wife throws their dead son's clothes into my yard, he knocks at the door to collect them all. My son, who in the practical sense would be the man of the house, says the whole thing is nutso, and he gets furious every time the Weimers start up with this mess, about every two weeks. We have to let him in, help collect the clothes, give the guy some pats on the back, nod along when he says the matter is nearly resolved, that none of this is all that terrible, and then, some five minutes after he's left, listen to her yelling again. My son thinks she shouts when she opens the closet and finds the boy's clothes there again.

"Are you fucking with me?" says my son every time this happens. "Next time I'm burning all the clothes." I unbolt the door and there is Weimer with his right palm on his forehead, almost covering his eyes, waiting for me to appear before he lowers his arm tiredly and apologizes with an "I don't want to bother you, but." I open the door and he comes in; he knows the way to the yard by now. There's fresh lemonade in the fridge, and I pour two glasses as he walks outside. Through the kitchen window I see him poke around in the grass and circle the geraniums, the area where the clothes usually land. When I go out I let the screen door slam to alert him, because there's something intimate about this act of collecting that I don't like to interrupt. I approach slowly. He straightens up with a sweater in his hand. There are more clothes draped over his other arm; he seems to have them all. "Who pruned the pines?" he asks. "My son," I say. "They look real good." He nods, gazing at them. They are three miniature trees, and my son tried to form cylindrical shapes, a little artificial, but original, it must be said. "Have some lemonade," I say. He drapes all the clothes over just one arm, and I hand him the glass. The sun isn't beating down yet, it's still early. I look sidelong at the bench we have a little farther on; it's made of concrete, and at this hour it's nice and warm, almost a panacea. "Weimer," I say, because I think it's friendlier than "Mr. Weimer." And I think, *Listen to me, throw those clothes away. That's all your wife wants.* But maybe he's the one who throws the clothes out the window and then regrets it, and it's the poor woman who's tormented every time she sees him carry them back in. Maybe they already tried to throw it all away in a big garbage bag, and the garbageman rang their doorbell to return it, same as what happened to us with my son's old clothes: "Ma'am, why don't you donate it. If I put this in the truck, it'll be no good to anyone." And there that bag is, still sitting in the laundry room; we definitely have to take it somewhere this week, I don't know where. Weimer is waiting, waiting for me. The light illuminates the sparse hair on his head, long and white, the silvery beard drawn faintly on his jaw, his eyes light but opaque, very small for the size of his face. I don't say anything, but I think Weimer guesses my thoughts. He lowers his eyes a moment. He sips more lemonade, looking now at his house, past the privet hedge that separates our yards. I search for something useful to say, something to confirm that I recognize his effort and to suggest some kind of solution, optimistic and imprecise. He looks back at me. He seems to intuit where this conversation that we haven't started is going, and he seems to gird himself to understand. "When something doesn't find its place . . ." I say, letting the final sounds hang in the air. Weimer nods once and waits. *My god*, I think, *we're in sync*. I'm in sync with this man who ten years ago returned my son's soccer balls deflated, this man who cut the flowers on my azaleas if they crossed the imaginary line that divided our properties. "When something doesn't find its place," I pick up again, looking at his clothes. "Tell me, please," says Weimer. "I don't know, but we have to move other things." *We have to make room*, I think, that's why it would be such a help to me if someone would take the bag I have in the laundry room. "Yes," says Weimer, clearly meaning "Go on." I hear the front door, a sound that means nothing to Weimer, but indicates to me that my son is home, safe and hungry. I take a long step toward the bench and sit down. I think that the warm concrete of the bench will also be a blessing for him, and I make room for him to join me. "Put down the clothes," I tell him. He doesn't seem to have any problem with this. He looks to either side for a place to leave them, and I think, *Weimer can do it, of course he can*. "Where?" he asks. "Leave them on the trees," I say, indicating the little pine trees, pruned into cylinders. Weimer obeys. He puts the clothes down and brushes the grass from his hands. "Have a seat." He sits. What do I do with this old man now? But there is something about him that encourages me to keep going. Something like having my hands under the running water, a calm that allows me to think of the words, organize the facts, consider things that always happen in the same order. Weimer's expectation seems to grow; one might almost say he was waiting for an instruction from me. It's a power and a responsibility and I can't figure out what to do with it. His light eyes grow damp: the final confirmation of this extraordinary synchronization. I look at him unabashedly, not leaving him any room for privacy, because I can't believe this is happening, and neither can I bear the weight it's exerting on me. I sit Weimer down and now I want to say something that will resolve this problem. I drink all of my lemonade and try to think of some sonorous and practical spell, a charm that would benefit us all, like "Buy my son as many balls as you deflated and everything will be fine," "If you cry without setting down your lemonade, she will stop throwing out the clothes," or "Leave the clothes on the pines for one night, and if the morning is clear, it means the problem will disappear." God, I could throw them out myself in the early morning hours while I'm smoking my last cigarette of the day. I'd have to mix them in with the trash so the garbageman wouldn't bring them back, and that's exactly what I should do with my son's clothes, it's got to be done this week. *Say something to solve this problem*, I repeat to myself so I don't lose focus. I've said things many times, and once uttered, the words brought about their effect. They kept my son with me, they ran my husband off, they arranged themselves divinely in my head every time I washed the dishes. In my yard, Weimer drinks the last drops from his glass and his eyes fill with tears, as if it were an effect of the lemon, and I think maybe it's too bitter for him, that maybe there's a moment when the effect no longer depends on our words, or when the impossible thing is their utterance. "Yes," Weimer said some long seconds ago, a yes that was a "go on," a "please," and now we are anchored together, the two empty glasses on the concrete bench, and on the bench our bodies. Then I have a vision, a wish: My son opens the screen door and walks toward us. His feet are bare, they step fast, they're young and strong over the grass. He is indignant with us, with the house, with everything that always happens in this house, always in the same way. His body grows toward us with a powerful energy that Weimer and I await without fear, almost eagerly. His enormous body that at times reminds me of my husband's and forces me to close my eyes. He's only a few meters away, now almost on top of us. But he doesn't touch us. I look again at my son and he veers off toward the small pines. He gathers the clothes furiously, wads them up in a ball and goes back the way he came, his body now distant and small, a silhouette. "Yes," says Weimer, and he sighs, and it's not the same yes as before. This is a more open, almost dreamy yes.

Breath from

the Depths

The list was part of a plan: Lola suspected that her life had been too long, so simple and light that now it lacked the weight needed to disappear. After studying the experiences of some acquaintances, she had concluded that even in old age, death needed a final push. An emotional nudge, or a physical one. And she couldn't give that to her body. She wanted to die, but every morning, inevitably, she woke up again. What she could do, on the other hand, was arrange everything in that direction, attenuate her own life, reduce its space until she eliminated it completely. That's what the list was about; that, and remaining focused on what was important. She turned to it when her attention wandered, when something upset or distracted her and she forgot what it was she was doing. It was a short list:

Classify everything.

Donate what is expendable.

Wrap what is important.

Concentrate on death.

If he meddles, ignore him.

The list helped her deal with her head, but she'd found no solution for the deplorable state of her body. She could no longer bear more than five minutes on her feet, and it wasn't just the problems with her spine she was struggling with. Sometimes her breathing changed and she needed to take in more air than normal. When that happened, she inhaled as much as she could, then exhaled with a rough, deep sound, so strange that she could never quite comprehend that it came from her. If she walked in the dark at night, from the bed to the bathroom and the bathroom to the bed, the sound was like an ancient being breathing on her neck. It was born in the depths of her lungs and came from an inexorable physical need. To mask it, Lola added a nostalgic whistle to the exhalation, a melody somewhere between bitter and resigned that had been taking root within her little by little. The list is what's important, she told herself every time the lethargy immobilized her. She couldn't care less about all the rest.

They ate breakfast in silence. He prepared everything, and he did it just the way Lola liked. Sliced wheat bread, two different fruits chopped into little pieces, mixed together, and divided again into a portion for each of them. In the center of the table were the sugar and the white cheese; beside her coffee mug, the low-calorie orange marmalade; next to his coffee mug, the candied sweet potato and the yogurt. The newspaper was his, but the sections on health and wellness were for her, and they were folded and placed beside her napkin for when she finished breakfast. If she looked at him with her butter knife in hand, he passed her the bread plate. If she stared off at a spot on the tablecloth, he let her be, because he knew that something more was happening, something he couldn't meddle in. She watched him chew, sip his coffee, turn the newspaper pages. She looked at his hands—so unmasculine now, white and fine with carefully filed nails—and the little hair left on his head. She didn't reach any great conclusion or make any decisions in that regard. She just looked at him and reminded herself of concrete facts that she never analyzed: *Fifty-seven years now, I've been married to this man. This is my life now.* When they finished breakfast, they carried the things to the sink. He brought the stool over, and she washed the dishes while sitting down. The stool allowed her to rest her elbows on the edge of the sink, so she hardly had to bend over. He would have gladly taken care of the dishes, but she didn't want to owe him anything, and he let her do it. Lola washed slowly, thinking about the TV schedule for that day, and about her list. She carried it twice-folded in the pocket of her apron. If it was unfolded, a white cross appeared in the center of the paper. She knew it would start to tear soon. Sometimes, on days like this one, Lola needed more time; she finished doing the dishes but didn't feel ready to continue with the rest of the day, so she spent a while scrubbing at the grime that had accumulated between the metal and the plastic of the small spoons, the rocks of damp sugar on the lid of the sugar bowl, the rusty base of the kettle, the limescale around the faucet.

Sometimes, too, Lola cooked. He brought the stool to the kitchen and set out everything she asked for. It's not that she couldn't move, she could if something important warranted it, but since her spine and her breathing made everything so difficult, she saved her strength for when he couldn't help her. He took care of the taxes, the garden, the shopping, and everything that went on outside the house. She made a list—another list, a shopping list—and he stuck to it. If he missed something, he had to go back out, and if there was something extra, she asked what it was and how much it had cost.

Sometimes he bought cocoa that came in a powder to mix with milk, like her son used to drink before he got sick. The son they'd had together had not grown any taller than the kitchen cabinets. He had died long before. In spite of everything that can be given and lost for a child, in spite of the world and all there is on the world's surface, in spite of her having thrown the crystal glasses from the cabinets to the floor and stepped on them barefoot and bloodied everything on the way to the bathroom, and from the bathroom to the kitchen, and from the kitchen to the bathroom, and so on until he arrived and managed to calm her. Since then, he's bought the smallest box of hot cocoa, the one with two hundred and fifty grams, the one that comes in a cardboard container, even though it's not the thriftiest option. It wasn't on her lists, but it was the only item she made no comment on. She just placed the box in the upper cabinet, behind the salt and the spices. And that was when she discovered that the box she had placed there a month earlier was gone. She never saw him use the powdered cocoa, really, she didn't know how it ever ran out, but it was a subject she preferred not to ask about.

They ate healthy products, which Lola chose attentively from what she saw on TV. Everything they ate for breakfast, lunch, or dinner had at some point appeared in an advertisement announcing vitamins, low calories, or the absence of genetically modified ingredients. In the rare instances when she added a new product to his list, she would search the grocery bags for it and then study it beside the window, in natural light. She was well versed in what a healthy product should or should not contain. There were good doctors and nutritionists advising people all about it on TV, like Dr. Petterson on the eleven o'clock show. If Lola found something suspicious or contradictory to the advertisements, she called the customer service number and asked to speak with someone in charge. Once, even though her complaints did not persuade the company to return her money, the next day she received a box with twenty-four peaches-and-cream yogurts. They had already bought their yogurts for that week, and the expiration dates seemed too close together. She would open the refrigerator and see the yogurts there, and the amount of space they took up made her anxious. They wouldn't be eaten in time, they would go bad, and she didn't know what to do with them. She mentioned it several times to him. She explained the complications, expecting him to understand that something had to be done about it, something that was no longer within her capabilities. One afternoon, the problem got the best of her. Nothing in particular happened, she just knew that she couldn't keep opening the fridge and seeing the yogurts still there. Her afternoon snack consisted only of coffee, and although later on she was secretly ashamed of her anger, she still felt indignant at having no prospects for any type of solution, no resources of her own with which to fight. When he finally took the yogurts away, she didn't ask any questions. She moved the stool to the fridge, where she propped the door open, and, sitting down, whistling slightly at abrupt movements to hide her gasping breath, she took the opportunity to clean the shelves and reorganize the things that remained.

It wasn't just what was on the news; she could learn a lot about the world from her kitchen window. The neighborhood had turned dangerous. It was poorer, dirtier. There were at least three empty houses on her street, with overgrown grass and mail piled up in the front yards. At night, only the streetlights on the corners worked, and with all the trees blocking them they weren't good for much. There was a group of young kids, surely drug addicts, who almost always sat on the curb just meters away from her house, and they stayed there until early morning. Sometimes they yelled or threw bottles, and a few days earlier they'd played a game where they ran from one end of her fence to the other, hitting the metal bars like a xylophone, and this was at night, when she was trying to sleep. From her bed, she hissed at him several times to get him to do something. He woke up and leaned against his headboard, but didn't go out and say anything to the kids. They sat in silence, listening.

"They're going to scratch the fence," she said.

"They're just kids."

"Kids scratching up our fence."

But he didn't move from his bed.

The matter of the fence was clearly related to the

arrival of the new neighbors. They had taken over the house next door to hers a week ago. They pulled up in a decrepit truck that sat in front of the house with its engine running for almost fifteen minutes before anything happened. Lola stopped what she was doing and waited at the window the whole time. She told herself she had to take precautions: the looks of this new family gave her no reason to think they had bought or rented the house. Finally, one of the truck doors opened. Lola let out a long wheeze and felt a bitter misgiving, as if, after a long hesitation over whether to ruin her day or not, they had finally chosen to do it. A thin woman got out. Seeing her from behind, Lola thought she might be a teenager, because her hair was long and loose and she was dressed very casually, but when the woman closed the door, Lola saw that she must be around forty. The engine turned off, and the same door opened again. A boy of around twelve, thirteen years old got out. And from the other side, a burly man dressed in blue overalls. They didn't have many belongings; maybe the house was already furnished. Lola caught sight of two single mattresses, a table, five chairs—none matching—and a dozen bags and suitcases. The boy took care of the loose items. The woman and man moved the rest, occasionally conferring about the best way to unload and move the things, until the truck was empty and the man left without a goodbye, just a wave of a hand before rolling up the window.

That night, Lola tried to talk to him, to make him understand the new problem that this move meant. They fought.

"Why do you have to be so prejudiced?"

"Because someone has to wear the pants in this house."

Behind Lola's house, the land sloped upward toward the back. He had divided up those final meters of land and planted two plum trees, two orange trees, a lemon tree, and a small kitchen garden with spice plants and tomatoes. He spent a few hours in the afternoons back there. When she looked out the kitchen window to call him, she saw him crouched down beside the wooden fence that separated their land from the neighbors'. He was talking to a boy who was listening from the other side of the fence. It could be the new neighbor boy, but she wasn't sure; it was hard to tell from her lookout. That night, over dinner, she waited for him to spontaneously clarify the situation. This was something new, and everything new should be mentioned. It was his responsibility to do it, and dinner was the appropriate time; that's why at night the TV was turned off and Lola asked, How was your day? So Lola waited. She listened to the familiar story about the friend from poker he often ran into at the bank. She listened to a comment about the supermarket, even though he knew very well that after her incident the last time she ever set foot there, she never wanted to hear a word about that hell again. She listened to the problem of the streets blocked off downtown because of the sewage system, and his predictable opinions about almost everything. But he didn't say anything about the boy, and she considered the possibility that this wasn't their first meeting in the backyard, and the thought alarmed her.

She kept watch for a few days and saw that it was the boy who ran toward him as soon as he went out to the garden, and not vice versa. Seeing them together made her uncomfortable, as if something wasn't right, just like the twenty-four peaches-and-cream yogurts taking up space in the fridge.

One afternoon the boy came over to their side of the fence and sat on a stool—*their* stool—while her husband went on working in the garden. The boy said something and the two of them laughed. Once, when she was there beside the window, behind the curtain, she thought about the cocoa powder and gave a start. She thought something could be escaping her, something she hadn't thought about until then. She went to the kitchen, opened the cabinet, moved the salt and the spices aside. The cocoa box was open, and there wasn't much left in it. She thought about taking it out, and then realized it wasn't such a simple action. The kitchen was her territory. Everything in the kitchen was organized according to her directives, and it was the area of the house where she had total control. But the cocoa powder was different. She touched the drawing on the package and looked out at the backyard. She couldn't do much more than that, and she didn't very well understand the meaning of what she was doing. She closed the cabinet door, then the kitchen door behind her. She went into the living room and sat in her armchair. Everything happened slowly, but as fast as her body would allow each movement. With her hands in her pockets, she caressed the list. It was good to know it was still there.

Sometimes, if the weather was dry and mild enough, she went out to the front yard to check on the impatiens, the Chinese lanterns, and the azaleas. He took care of most of the house's watering needs, but the flowerbeds in front were what could best be seen from the street, and they needed special care. So she made an effort and monitored the flowers and the dampness of the soil. That morning, the woman and the boy passed by on the sidewalk. The woman nodded in greeting, but Lola couldn't bring herself to respond. She stood there and watched them go by, weighted down by coats and backpacks. She needed to evaluate this new situation, the problem it would now pose to go out and check on the plants at that hour, the constant possibility of interruption. She needed more air, and she took a deep breath and let it out with a wheeze, controlling the speed just as the doctor had taught her. She went back inside the house, bolted the door, and dropped into her armchair. She knew it was a dangerous situation. She concentrated on the rhythm of her breathing, on slowing it down. A moment later she fumbled under her body for the remote control and turned on the TV. On top of everything, she thought, she had to move forward with her list, she had to go on classifying and wrapping, and she didn't have much time left. She knew she was going to die, and she'd implied as much to the lady from the rotisserie when she called to place her order on nights when she didn't have the energy to cook. She had also talked about it with the soda man when he brought the replacement five liters of mineral water for the dispenser in the kitchen. She explained to them why she breathed like that, the matter of pulmonary oxygenation, and the risks and consequences it entailed. Once, she showed the soda man her list, and he'd seemed impressed.

But something wasn't working: everything kept going. Why, when her intentions were so clear, did her body wake up again every day? It was a cruel and unusual thing, and Lola was starting to fear the worst: that death required an effort she could no longer make.

A few years earlier, when she was still the one who went to the supermarket, she'd found a hand cream in the skincare aisle that left almost no residue. It really did have aloe vera in it; she could smell it every time she uncapped the tube. She'd spent a fair amount of time—and money—trying out brands before she found it. These days, she had him buy a different cream, one that cost less than half as much and was very bad. She could have asked him to buy the other one without offering any explanation, but then he would know she had once spent that kind of money on lotion. That was the sort of thing she sometimes missed. Because she would never go back to the supermarket, no matter how much he insisted on talking about it at dinner, knowing perfectly well that she hated listening. Never, not after the incident, not after that disastrous day at the grocery store. It was one of the few things she remembered clearly, and it filled her with shame. Did he remember it, too? Did he know only what he'd seen when he arrived? Or had the witnesses eventually told him everything?

She looked at the clock and saw it was three in the morning. He was breathing in the other bed. Not snoring, but his breaths were deep and distracting, and she knew right away she wouldn't be able to get back to sleep. She lay awake and waited until she felt strong enough. She put on her robe, went to the bathroom, and sat on the toilet a good while. She thought about some of the things she could do, like wash her face or brush her teeth or hair, but she understood it wasn't about any of those things. She left the bathroom and went to the kitchen, walking down the hall without turning on the lights, sensing the shelf with his *National Geographic*s, and the dresser with the sheets and towels. She went to the front door, then wondered why she might have gone there. In the kitchen, she picked up the matches and lit one of the burners. Then she turned it off. She turned on the fluorescent light under the upper cabinets and opened some to be sure the provisions were up-to-date. She moved the spices, and there was the new box of cocoa powder, unopened. She felt her breathing change slightly and she felt, stronger than ever, the need to do something, but she couldn't understand exactly what. She leaned against the counter and breathed calmly. Outside, the front yard was in darkness; one of the two streetlights had burned out. She saw the car, and at the neighbors' house across from her the lights were out. A shadow moved in the street, and then a few seconds later, in her yard, behind the tree outside the kitchen.

Breath from the Depths

Lola held her breath. She took a quick step backward, reached her hand to the wall, and turned out the light. Her body responded to this emergency with agility and without pain, but she chose not to dwell on that. She stood still in the dark, staring at the tree. She waited like that for a while, gradually letting her breath out until the wheeze returned and she was convinced no one was out there. Then she saw, against the black tree trunk, in silhouette, someone who was trying to stay hidden. Someone was there, no doubt about it. And she was alone in the kitchen, struggling with her body and her breathing, while he was off sleeping peacefully. She stood thinking about that for a moment, so close to the cocoa powder that she could have reached it without moving her feet. So it occurred to her that it could be the boy from next door. She opened the window a crack. The dog from across the street barked behind the fence. The black trunk was motionless for several seconds. She took five steps back to the kitchen door, from where she could still see the tree, then picked up the receiver for the intercom and pressed the talk button. Her own hoarse whistle reached her from the yard, wafting in through the open window. She hung the receiver up and stood with her hand trembling on the device, until, a while later, the dog stopped barking.

◻

It was hot out on the day of the supermarket incident. There are things Lola no longer remembers, but she knows that for sure. She fainted because of the heat, not because of what happened. The doctor, the ambulance, it all seemed excessive, a humiliation that could have been avoided. She would have expected the cashier and the security guard, both women who had known her for years and who waved to her at least twice a week, to have more solidarity, but they looked on in silence, rapt and stupid as if they'd never seen such a thing. Other customers— some she knew by sight, some of them neighbors—saw her on the floor and then on the stretcher. Lola wasn't a chatty person, she didn't have a real friendship with any of those people, and she wouldn't really have wanted one. That's why it was all so embarrassing, because she would never get the chance to explain herself. She grew bitter if she thought about that, and more bitter still when she remembered the details, like how she closed her eyes while they loaded her into the ambulance so she wouldn't see how the two men in the delivery truck parked outside the store were staring. Her husband and the doctors made her spend two days in the hospital for routine tests. They subjected her to analyses and exams and never once asked her opinion. They came with their forms and their explanations, falsely solicitous, imposing on her time and her patience, efficiently invoicing for as many medical procedures as possible. She knew how those things worked, but she didn't get a voice or a vote; it was all up to him, and he was so naive and obsequious. It's true there are things that Lola doesn't remember, but she remembers that perfectly.

Someone had been in the front yard the night before. She told him as soon as he woke her up: she'd fallen asleep in front of the muted TV, and now two women were cooking a chicken in a bright, spacious kitchen. Her armchair usually seemed quite comfortable, but that time it hadn't worked. Her body hurt and it was hard to move. He didn't ask if she'd spent the night there or what had happened, but he did want to know if she'd taken her pills. She didn't answer. He went for the pill case and brought it to her with a glass of water. He stood looking at her until she'd finished swallowing them. After the last sip, she said:

"I'm telling you that someone was in the front yard last night. You should check to be sure everything is okay."

He looked toward the yard.

"Are you sure?"

"I saw him, behind the tree."

He put on his jacket and went outside. She watched him from the window, saw him walk down the log path that led to the gate, stop even with the tree, and look out toward the street from there. It seemed to her that he was consciously not checking what she had told him to. He didn't do anything right, and she thought how this man had been that way his whole life, and now she depended on this very same man. She picked up the intercom handset, the one in the living room beside the door, and she heard her own voice coming from the speaker outside:

"The tree, the tree."

She saw him take a few steps toward the tree, but he didn't get close enough. He glanced around and came back.

"You should look again," she said when he came inside. "I'm sure I saw someone."

"There's no one now."

"But there was last night," she said, and she let her lungs whistle lengthily in resignation.

She'd spent part of the morning labeling the five visible sides of the boxes that were already sealed. He stuck his head into the guest room, looked at the pile of boxes, and offered to take them to the garage. He said that way the room would still be usable, and plus, when the time came, it would be much easier to load out the boxes from the garage.

"Load them out?" she said. "And take them where? I'm the only one who's going to decide which boxes go."

He could take them to the garage if that made him so happy, but she would let him take only the expendable boxes. The important things would always stay inside the house.

She never packed up more than one box a day, and she didn't pack one every day. Sometimes she only classified items, or thought about what she should do the next day. But this time, it was old winter clothes. She had already spent an arduous two weeks putting the ruined ones into trash bags, and he had taken them away, one by one, when he drove downtown or to the supermarket. That day, Lola was working with the last sweaters to be donated. They were wool and took up a lot of room, so she put them into two boxes that she taped shut. Sealing two boxes gave her a strange feeling of vertigo that she didn't really know how to handle. She looked out the window. She forgot what she'd been doing, but then she opened the list and remembered. She went to ask him to take a chair outside for her, to the front yard. He was folding and putting away the towels he had taken off the clothesline, and he stood looking at her for a moment.

"I don't have to explain to you why I need a chair outside. I need it there, period."

He set the towels on the counter and looked at her again. She was wearing her pajamas, a pink jacket, and the felt slippers that were torn from so much use but always clean, and she held her list and a pen.

"Where do you want the chair?" he asked.

"On the porch, looking toward the street."

She followed him to be sure he took the right chair and that he didn't bang the cedar door on the way outside. She waited for him to leave and angled the chair toward the sun. She half fell with a loud whistle at the end and a slight grunt of pain that she dragged out a few seconds before leaning back into the chair. She unfolded her list, but didn't read it over. It was nearly noon, and the woman and boy would soon pass by the front door. She focused on the wait and then, gradually, dozed off.

One afternoon when her husband had gone downtown to run a few errands, the boy rang the bell. She peered out the kitchen window and recognized him immediately. He was with another boy his age on the other side of the gate. They were talking in low voices. She didn't know whether to answer or not. She looked at the clock and saw that he should be home any minute. When the doorbell rang again, she made a decision and picked up the intercom receiver. She rested a bit before speaking. She was agitated. As always, the sound of her breathing preceded her voice in the yard, and the boys looked at each other, amused.

"Yes . . ." said Lola.

"Ma'am, I'm here to return something of your husband's."

"What do you have to return?"

The boys looked at each other. Lola saw the neighbor boy had something in his hand, but she couldn't see what it was.

"A tool."

"Come back later."

The other boy said something rude under his breath.

"Come on, ma'am, let us in," said the neighbor.

The other boy had something in his hand as well, something long and heavy.

"Come back later."

She hung up the receiver and stayed where she was. She could see them out the kitchen window, but they probably couldn't see her.

"Hey, lady, don't be like that," yelled the other boy, and he hit the fence three times with whatever was in his hand.

Lola recognized the sound from the other night. The boys waited. When they saw she wasn't going to let them in, they left, and she stayed beside the intercom a while, listening to her breathing gradually grow steady. She told herself everything was fine, that it had only been a conversation through the intercom, but she didn't like those boys. Those boys could . . . She stood thinking for another moment; she knew she was close to something, something that hadn't yet taken shape but that, in its intensity—she knew very well how her own head worked—was becoming a premonition. Then, suddenly, she brought her hand to her heart and heard the first sound, coming from the other end of the house. She went toward the bedroom watching her feet advance, careful of her speed, containing her nerves so her breathing wouldn't quicken too much. She knew it was them. She needed to control her body. She was certain, and even so, when she reached the bedroom and saw them out the window, now almost inside her backyard, she was as startled as if the possibility had never occurred to her. They were at the back, ducking under the wire where the boy entered the vegetable garden. Lola hid to one side of the window. She saw them come toward the house and stop just a few meters away, now very close to her. They pushed on the garage door and found it was open—the garage was his, and it was his responsibility to lock it. Fear immobilized her. She heard the drawers in the metal cabinets opening and closing. They seemed like loud, strident noises. She thought about how she would make him understand that it was his fault they'd gotten in, that that boy he wasted his time with in the garden was a thief. Her breathing grew louder. She was afraid they would hear her, but it wasn't something she could help. There were more noises in the garage, then the door again. She saw them leave through the backyard and go under the fence toward the other house, but she couldn't see very well if they'd taken anything. She lay on the bed, put her feet under the blanket, and curled up in the fetal position. It would take a while for her heartbeat to normalize, but she would wait it out in that position so he would understand right away that she was not well. She decided that, whatever he asked her, she wouldn't say anything. If she could wait, there would be a perfect moment to bring this up, a moment she would recognize immediately. And she decided something else, too. That the days were growing more complicated and she shouldn't overextend herself: she would take a break from the matter of the boxes.

Lola remembered the doctor at the hospital perfectly. Though she didn't know his name, she'd be able to pick him out in a crowd from meters away. He wasn't at all like Dr. Petterson; there was a reason one of them worked on TV and the other at a third-rate medical insurer—the insurer her husband had chosen for the two of them when they retired.

"How's our patient feeling today?" That's what the hospital doctor asked on the three or four occasions he came to see her at home. He was always overheated—Lola could smell his sweat, something she did not consider hygienic in a doctor. But it was the question he asked that bothered her most. Clearly addressing her husband, trusting only his opinion, when *she* was the one he was treating. Sometimes Lola imagined herself leaping spryly from her armchair and saying something like "You two take care of this, I have things to do." But they needed her for the show. That's what she always told herself, and she remembered that, with him, half her life consisted of having patience.

"How's our patient feeling today?" Her lungs hurt, she had terrible back pain, her spleen stabbed her every time she stepped a little more quickly than she should, but none of that mattered to this doctor. His question was about something else. Something that had nothing to do with Lola's health. If she had listed all of her problems to Dr. Petterson, he would have been shocked at her untreated calamities, and he would have looked for some kind of solution. But these two men who were looking at her now—this doctor and *him*, especially him—were only interested in the supermarket incident and everything related to it. Symptoms before the incident, the results of the tests at the hospital, consequences of the incident. Incident.

The woman from the rotisserie told her once that it wasn't good to worry, that she had to try to be more optimistic. People tended to tell her things like that, and Lola liked to hear them. She knew none of it was going to help, because she was facing something worse than death, too complicated to explain over the phone. But it was a nice gesture on the woman's part: even if it didn't help in the slightest, her patience made Lola feel better.

In the following days the boy came over with the folding stool—*their* stool—under his arm. He unfolded it and sat down to watch her husband work, or sometimes her husband rested a little while they talked. Once, he pretended he was digging into the boy's stomach with his garden spade, and the boy laughed. During those days Lola paid special attention to whether or not he increased the ration of cocoa powder when he went shopping, but it stayed the same. She also took notice of the silences during their dinners. But he never said anything about it. Sometimes the omission soothed her; it relegated the matter of the boy to a lesser place, and she wondered if maybe it was a passing private obsession. Until she saw the boy out there again the next morning, and again her breathing rang out in the living room like a guttural alarm contained between the picture windows.

One night, things aligned in her favor: there was a robbery at the rotisserie. She found out from him, after he went to pick up dinner. Lola didn't call the woman who took the orders; she decided it wasn't appropriate, in spite of the intimacy that had grown from their conversations about her death. So they were dining on chicken again, and he was talking about the robbery. It was a good moment to ask about the boy, to subvert the silence he'd been subjecting her to: when he thought back to the conversation he wouldn't be able to pinpoint the trap, he would find only the subject of the rotisserie, which he himself had brought up. She waited patiently. He talked about the gun the rotisserie woman kept under the shelf, about the wounds on her arm and the ambulance that had come. He said the woman had been very brave, explained why he thought her daughter—who also worked at the rotisserie—hadn't been as good under pressure, how long it took the police to arrive, and how they'd interrogated the witnesses. Lola listened in silence, accustomed to waiting for him. Every three or four of his sentences, she would rewrite everything mentally in a single line, clear and concise, silently correcting his exasperating slowness. She forgave him. Then there was a silence, a long one, and she said:

"So what about the boy from next door? You think he had anything to do with it?"

"Why would he be involved?"

"They're the ones who bang on the fence. Him and another boy. They came by the other day and wanted to come in and return a tool of yours." Lola wanted to stop, mete out the information, but now the whole problem was on her shoulders and she couldn't stand so much weight; she had to drop it. "I didn't let them in, but they came in anyway, from the back. They were in the garage, they went through your things. You didn't lock the door. You should see if the drill and the soldering iron are still there."

"The drill and the soldering iron?"

She nodded, controlled her breathing. Until she put it into words, she hadn't really thought about the drill and the soldering iron, but they both knew those were his most expensive tools. He glanced toward the garage, and she realized she had managed to alarm him. She imagined him going through the tools and listing the ones that were missing while she found the number for the police station in her phone book. But he picked up his silverware again, raised another bite of chicken to his mouth, and said:

"The fixed wrench."

He had to say something more, so Lola just looked at him.

"For the kitchen sink. His mother asked for it and I lent it to them."

"And you didn't tell me."

"It was several days ago. When they moved in."

"The day they moved in."

"Yes," he said. "That day."

Lola waited until he was in the shower to check the garage herself, but she realized she couldn't remember what tools he had or where they were kept. Nor did she know exactly what a fixed wrench was. And since the garage was the only part of the house under his management, she suspected that everything would be dirty and disorganized. She wondered if he could be covering for the boy for some reason, and it didn't seem like an idea she could rule out. She felt for the list in her apron pocket, and thought that she would have to recall the facts and analyze them more calmly later that night. Make some kind of decision.

The next morning she put together another box. She filled it with old office supplies: dried-out pens, notebooks with yellowed pages, boxes of worn-out rubber bands, telephone books from past years. She was sure poor people would find those things useful, if only to know they exist, in case someday they came to need them. She went to the small office space he had set up on the phone table to organize bills and packed up some other things she found there. She wanted to also wrap the small ceramic Greek bust he used as a paperweight on the living room table, but she couldn't find it. She knew sometimes she didn't remember everything she had packed up. There were too many things and it was all on her shoulders, so it was only logical that details would escape her at times. The week before, they'd had to open a box because, in a moment of distraction, all of his shoes had been packed up. There were few towels, and the big mirror in the hallway no longer looked as good now that the table was empty. Nor were there any brushes or combs in her drawers in the bathroom. That was the worst, to find herself forced to always use his old comb.

At noon she taped up the box, stuck on a label, and wrote *Office Supplies*. She went to look for him so he could carry the box to the garage, but she didn't find him in any room of the house. Nor was he in the garage or the garden—she could see that from her bedroom window. They had agreed he wouldn't leave the house without telling her, because that kind of disappearance was precisely what made her the most nervous. She might need him, and she had to be able to count on him at all times. She crossed the living room and opened the front door. She saw him on the ground, and her breathing almost hiccuped before the wheeze. She clutched the doorframe. He was sitting with his back against the wall and his forehead in the palm of his hand. Lola took in enough air and strength to say: "My god!"

And he said:

"I'm okay, don't be scared." He looked at his bloodied palm; there was a small cut on his forehead. "I think my blood pressure dropped, but I caught myself."

"I'll call a doctor."

"Later. For now I need to go inside and lie down."

She prepared the bed for him. Brought him a cup of tea. Found the two latest issues of *National Geographic* on the hallway bookshelf and set them on the nightstand. She focused on doing all this at a logical speed: as quickly as possible, but without letting the movements agitate her. She was aware that this "moment" was his, and she had to do certain things to relieve him. But, frightened as he was, he might think only of himself, and someone had to go on taking care of her. It was an intense thing, in its own way. And Lola was up to it.

Then he fell asleep. She walked to the living room with a final effort and sat down in her armchair to rest. She had to recover her strength—there was still a lot to do.

She woke up to the sound of pipes banging on the fence. She craned her neck to look out the window, but a cramp forced her back into her initial position. Although there was no one in sight, she knew who it was. The clock above the TV said 4:20 in the afternoon. She heard the neighbor's high heels walking on her sidewalk toward the house next door. Then a door closing. She thought about the fixed wrench. She balled her hands into fists and stretched her arms out to the sides. It was an exercise from Dr. Petterson's program that she used to stretch and loosen up. The cramp dissipated and she felt she could once again depend on her body, or at least part of it. In her imagination, she tried to bring the uncertain shape of the wrench into focus. She checked to be sure she was wearing the red felt slippers and that her cool-weather jacket hung from the coat rack in the entryway, beside the intercom. It encouraged her to see that the objects were arranged in her favor. She stood up, put her jacket on, and opened the front door. That's how she finally understood what her intentions were, and it seemed to her that, clearly, this was a very sensible solution.

She went to the house next door and knocked. By the time the woman finally opened, much of the energy from her nap had been expended in the wait. Now everything would be more difficult. The woman recognized her right away and invited her in. Lola accepted with a half smile. She took a few steps and stopped, unable to decide what to do or say next.

"Would you like some tea?" asked the woman, and she walked toward the kitchen. "Have a seat if you like," she called from the other room. "Please excuse the mess."

The walls were peeling. There was almost no furniture except for a table, three rickety chairs, and two armchairs covered in sheets that were transparent from use, knotted around the armrests so they wouldn't slip off. The woman came back with a cup of tea and invited her to sit in one of the armchairs. They looked uncomfortable and Lola thought it would be hard to get up, but she accepted out of politeness. The woman moved quickly and brought a chair over for Lola to use as a table. Then Lola saw the magazines and papers piled on the floor beside the window. They took up a lot of space, and surely had no use.

"I have boxes if you want," said Lola. "They're strong boxes, I use them to pack up and classify things."

The woman followed Lola's gaze to her piles of papers.

"No need, thank you. But tell me, what can I do for you? Is it about my son? He didn't come home last night and I'm very worried."

Lola immediately understood the precision of her intuitions, and she remembered the noise of the fence from earlier that day. The woman was waiting for some kind of sign. She sat down in the other armchair, across from Lola.

"I think he's mad at me. Please, do you know anything?"

Lola was on the right path, but she had to move forward carefully.

"No. It's not that. I have to ask you an important question."

Lola looked at the tea and told herself that this had to come out right.

"I need to know if you have a wrench. A fixed wrench."

The woman frowned.

"The kind you use to fix sinks," said Lola.

Maybe the woman wasn't sure whether or not she had the wrench, maybe she didn't understand the question. She looked toward the kitchen, then turned back to Lola.

"I know what you're referring to, your husband lent us something like that last week. My son returned it the day before yesterday. He did return it, didn't he?"

"That's the problem. I'm not sure."

The woman stared at her for a moment.

"It's just that it's very important for me to know where that wrench is." Lola stirred her tea and removed the bag. "It's not about the wrench, I'm sure you understand. I mean, I'm looking for the wrench, but not *for* the wrench."

The woman nodded once and seemed to be making an effort to understand. Lola looked toward the kitchen and sat a few seconds in silence, until she heard a voice talking to her.

"Do you feel all right?"

She had completely forgotten her aches and pains. Her breathing was almost silent, and all her energy was projected toward an as yet unknown physical space, toward the natural light that came from the kitchen and opened toward them.

"What's your name?" asked Lola.

"Susana."

The woman had very dark circles under her eyes that pulled them downward in a way that looked artificial.

"Susana, would you mind if I had a look at your kitchen?"

"Do you think I wouldn't return the wrench? What kind of person do you think I am?"

"Oh, no, no, no. Don't misunderstand me. This is about something else. It's . . . How can I explain? It's a premonition, that's what it is."

The woman seemed annoyed, but she stood up, walked toward the kitchen, and waited for Lola in the doorway. Lola set her mug on the chair, got to her feet with the help of the armrests, picked up the mug again, and walked toward her.

It was a bright, spacious kitchen, and although the cabinets were shabby, some fruit and a few red pots and pans lent the room a pleasant warmth. Lola thought that if it were cleaned and organized, the place could look even more inviting than her own kitchen. Inadvertently, she took in more air than necessary and exhaled with a whistle. She knew the woman was looking at her, and she was ashamed. She thought of him—he might have woken up, and he would be scared if he couldn't find her in the house.

"What are you looking for, ma'am?" The woman was not hostile; her voice just sounded tired.

Lola turned to look at her. They were very close to each other, each leaning against one side of the doorway.

"There's something else I have to ask you."

"Go ahead."

"It might seem strange, but . . ."

The woman crossed her arms as they looked at each other, and she no longer seemed quite so receptive.

"Do you think someone could be giving chocolate milk to your son?"

"Come again?"

Lola looked at her own yard through the window. She needed to breathe more air, and she started to wheeze in agitation, as quietly as possible.

"Chocolate milk," said Lola, "powdered cocoa." She realized she was no longer controlling her breathing, and she heard the whistle ring out in the kitchen.

"I don't understand," said the woman.

Something happened with her vision, as if the whiteness of the walls grew more intense. Her heart pounded in her chest and Lola whistled again, a dry, horrendous sound. When she tried to set the tea on the table, her heart thumped once more, and she fainted.

She was breathing again, but the relief was only physical. In the darkness of her closed eyes she understood that she was still alive, when it would have been such a good moment to die. It hadn't happened this time, either. She had summoned death in many ways, but nothing worked. It was clear that she was missing something vital, and she really couldn't think of what else to do. She opened her eyes. She was in her room, but in his bed. The *National Geographic*s were right where she had left them. She called to him. There were sounds from the kitchen, his heavy footsteps, and she saw him appear in the bedroom doorway.

"I fainted," she said.

"But you're okay." He came in and sat down on the other bed—hers.

"I'm not in my bed."

"We thought you'd be better off farther from the window."

"We?"

"The neighbor caught you when you fell, and she helped me get you home."

"The boy's mother?"

She looked at the palm of her hand. There was a small cut.

"You don't remember anything? You walked here."

Lola didn't know what to say. She did remember, but would have liked to hear the story. At least now he wasn't the one in bed, and things were back to their natural order. She looked at the cut on her hand again, pressing the wound a little to see how much it hurt.

"And the boy? Did she find him?"

"No," he said.

She thought about the woman, about their interrupted conversation, about the fixed wrench and the chocolate milk, and an inner alarm went off again. She tried to stand up, but didn't have the strength. He helped her by placing another pillow behind her. She didn't share her concerns with him, but she let him do it.

⬜

There were things Lola didn't remember, but the super-market incident was intact in her mind. The incident, and the visits from that useless doctor who always asked: "How's our patient feeling today?" And he asked it looking at him, because neither of them expected her to answer. What was it that idiot still needed to find out?

Sometimes, when he asked that question, she felt twinges in her spleen even though she hadn't made any sudden movements, and she knew that her breathing would soon grow agitated and start to resound in the bedroom.

"It would be good for you to keep a list," the doctor told her once.

What a brilliant man, thought Lola. If her hands shook, she folded them in her lap so he couldn't see them.

"A list of what? I remember everything perfectly," said Lola, and she saw the two men exchange a glance.

They talked to her like she was stupid because neither of them was man enough to tell her she was dying. She knew that wasn't true—she wasn't dying—but sometimes she liked to fantasize about the idea. He deserved it: if she died, he would understand how important she had been for him, all the years she had been at his service. She wanted to die so badly, she'd wanted it for so many years, and yet her body just went on deteriorating, more than she would have thought possible. A deterioration that led nowhere. Why didn't they tell her? She wanted them to say it. She wanted so badly for it to be true.

Lola opened her eyes. His clock said 3:40 and she was sure she'd heard a sound. She wondered if this was another intruder, like that night when someone had come into the front yard, even though he couldn't find any traces the next morning. She stood up slowly so as not to wake him—this was clearly something she would have to resolve on her own—put on her slippers and robe, and went down the hall. The sound came again, and now she could hear it clearly. It was a tapping at the bathroom window. Lola thought it could be pebbles hitting the frosted glass. She went in without turning on the light, sliding along the wall to reach the window, and waited. It happened two more times, and she was sure this was the boy. She went back to the bedroom and cracked the window. It was a strategic position, and at the fifth sound she thought she could tell where the pebbles were coming from. A few meters off toward the end of the house, under the fence and the privet hedge that separated her yard from the woman's, there was a small ditch. And someone was in the ditch, lying down. It was the boy who was throwing pebbles; she couldn't see him, but she knew. Were the pebbles meant to call her husband? Lola shifted her weight to the other leg so her feet wouldn't ache. Why did she have to put up with these things, at her age? And he wasn't about to go outside at this hour, not by any means; it was dangerous and it was stupid. He had no business with that boy. She had to forget about the problem of the boy, that's what, she told herself several times, reminding herself as well about the list, and with it, all the things she still had left to do.

Maybe because she hadn't slept well, things happened more slowly than usual that day. She had trouble moving from one place to another, raising her voice to call him, making the list for the supermarket. But she managed it, somehow. He helped her. Not enough, but he did contribute. He took care of breakfast, turned on the TV for her. Brought her slippers. She watched Dr. Petterson's show. Unfolded and refolded the paper with the list several times. For her nap, she decided to go back to bed. She had him change the sheets, and he knew where to leave the dirty ones and which of the clean sheets he should use, all without her having to tell him. They slept soundly and got up well rested. He brought more boxes. The three he'd gotten the previous week were already packed and labeled in the garage. She saw him look at the piles and frown. He seemed to wonder what the point was in packing so many boxes, but of course that was a question he could never answer for himself, just as he couldn't say why it was necessary to throw products out after their expiration dates even if they still smelled good, or hang the clothes neatly on the line even though they'd still have to be ironed later. Those details were outside his grasp, and she had to shoulder them entirely. His frown at the boxes could be merely the expression of a passing thought about the garden or the car. She waited for him, standing behind him. Lola was so used to waiting for him. And yet, something alarmed her: the way he leaned over to read the labels. Not because of what was written on the labels or the boxes. What alarmed her was his sudden interest. He turned around and looked at her. She tried to think of something to say. She remembered there was another packed box in the bathroom and she could ask him to carry it out. She could ask him to go to the supermarket; she'd left the grocery list on the TV. There were many things she could have asked him for, but she couldn't decide on one. Then he said:

"The boy is missing."

She understood the close relationship this bore to her own personal desires, and for a moment she felt guilty.

"He didn't go home last night either, and it's almost noon now."

She thought about the robbery at the rotisserie, about the banging on the fence, the fixed wrench, the chocolate milk, and the stool the boy sat on in the garden, *their* stool. But she said:

"Isn't there anything of yours you want to box up?"

He turned toward the boxes and then back to her.
"Like what?"

"When my aunt died, my mother spent a year packing up boxes. We can't leave everything in other people's hands."

He looked out toward the garden and she thought he couldn't have much more than that, and she was afraid she'd hurt him. It was possible that a man like him didn't have enough things to fill a box.

"Do you think something happened to him?" he asked without taking his eyes from the garden. "Sometimes he comes over to our side around this time."

She balled up her fists and then opened them, hiding her impulse. The wound throbbed in the palm of her hand. It was done: he had said it. He had finally named the boy, and in such a distracted way that she hadn't been able to react in the appropriate way. *Him and the boy.* The news was implicit in his statement, "The boy is missing." He had been seeing the boy, out in the garden, all this time. He had done it knowing that she knew, and he hadn't been able to say it. He'd put it all out on the table, the boy's whole body that was his alone and that he'd hidden from her until now. She sucked in air and let her breathing surround them. She picked up the packing tape from atop the stack of boxes and walked toward the kitchen, gathering the necessary strength for what would come next.

He did some things in the bedroom and the hallway. She started in on the desk and took care of the last drawer in the closet. But the noises he was making weren't his usual ones; she could tell he was doing something out of the ordinary. It was concerning, and she would rather have taken a look and seen what was going on. He wasn't good with things around the house, he often needed some kind of guidance, but he'd said that thing about the boy and now she had to keep her distance. He needed to understand he had behaved poorly. So she held back. She let him be, and didn't say anything when she heard him go outside. He spent the rest of the afternoon in the garden, and came in at dusk. She saw him walking back carrying the stool and a few garden tools, and since she had already ordered dinner, she went to the living room to keep their paths from crossing. She turned on the TV and sat in her armchair to watch the news while he put the things in the garage. She dozed a little, then he came in. She heard the garage door and then the kitchen door. She heard him stop behind her, two meters away, and in that position, without taking her eyes from the TV, she waited for him to speak. She was sure he wanted to say something, and she imagined him searching for the words to apologize. She gave him time. She thought about taking the list from her pocket and looking it over, but a new sound forced her to catch her breath. A thump on the wooden floor. A muffled blow comprising several thumps. She turned and saw his body on the floor. He was bent in a strange, unnatural way, as if something inside him had deactivated suddenly, without leaving his body time to fall. A moment later she saw the fine trickle of blood spreading across the floor.

Lola called the rotisserie woman. The rotisserie woman sent an ambulance, and the ambulance driver, at the doctor's request, called the police. They took the body away wrapped in a gray bag. She asked to go with him in the ambulance, but the two policemen insisted she stay; they sat her in her armchair, and while one of them asked questions and took notes, the other went to the kitchen to make her some tea. Lola listened to the interrogation in a silence punctuated by sounds from the kitchen, the kettle on the burner, the cupboard doors opening and closing. She felt tired and, narrowing her eyes, she thought some things. There was the cocoa powder behind the salt and spices. There was the possibility that he still hadn't come back in from the garden, that the thud of his bones was part of some memory left over from the afternoon nap and he was still behind her, waiting. Several times she almost fell asleep, and she didn't care about the policeman who was repeating her name, or about the other officer in the kitchen. But over and over she heard the sound of bones hitting the floor behind her, and a sharp pain in her chest roused her, forced her to breathe. With resentful clarity, she understood that this would keep her alive forever. That he had died right under her nose, without any effort, and he'd left her alone with the house and the boxes. He had abandoned her forever, after all she had done for him. He'd said that thing about the boy and then gone to the grave with everything inside. Now she didn't even have anyone to die for. She let out her cavernous breath, deep and rough in the living room, and the policeman stopped talking and peered at her worriedly. The other one was beside her, holding the cup of tea. They insisted she couldn't be alone, and Lola understood she would have to think for a moment, return to reality, and get these men out of the house. She breathed and avoided making noise, bringing everything inward again. She lied and said there was a woman who took care of them, and she would come first thing the next day. She said she needed to sleep. The policemen left. She went to the kitchen to get the stool he used to put by the sink when she washed dishes. It was the only piece of furniture she was capable of moving on her own. She carried it to the living room and placed it against the wall, near where he had fallen. She sat and waited. The police had pushed the furniture aside and cleaned. In front of her, the floor was a damp, empty place, shining like an ice rink.

When it started to get dark, her back was aching and a fierce tingling was rising up her legs. She took her hands from her pockets, and there was the list. The list said:

Classify everything.

Donate what is expendable.

Wrap what is important.

Concentrate on death.

If he meddles, ignore him.

She understood that some things would change and that she wouldn't know what decisions to make, but that, unfairly, her breath would remain, filling her lungs. She tried to straighten her body to see if it would still respond. The list had eighteen words, and she paid close attention to every one of them. Then she took out her pen and crossed out the last line.

At some point in the night she went into the bedroom to lie down. She was about to fall asleep when the doorbell rang. Her head was working slowly, but in its own time it alerted her that this was something different and dangerous. She got up holding on to the edge of the bed and went back to the living room without turning on the lights. She heard a thud from outside and thought again about the sound of bones. The exhaustion stunned her, relieved the fear. She peered out the peephole in the front door. Behind the gate, a dark shadow was waiting beside the intercom. It was the boy. He was clutching his right arm with his left hand, as if he were in pain or had been wounded. He rang the doorbell again. Lola picked up the receiver and breathed.

"Open up, please," said the boy, "open up."

He was looking to his right toward the corner, and he seemed genuinely frightened.

"Where is the drill?" asked Lola. "Do you think he didn't realize the drill is missing?"

The boy looked toward the corner again.

"Can I go into the garage?" He made a sound of pain that seemed fake to Lola. "Can I talk to him?"

Lola hung up the receiver and went to the garage as fast as she could. Her body, charged with adrenaline, was up to the task. She locked the back door and the windows. Then she went to the bedroom and locked the windows there, too. The doorbell rang again, and again, and again. And then it didn't ring anymore.

The police called the next morning. A kid from administration had orders to make sure everything was okay. He apologized when he realized he'd woken her up. He told her the body was at the morgue and they would deliver it that afternoon. If she wanted, she could contract a funeral service for Saturday morning and they would bring the body there. Lola hung up and went to the kitchen. She opened the fridge and closed it again. She saw it was time for Dr. Petterson's show, so she went into the living room and sat down, but didn't have the strength to turn on the TV.

He had left a box. Lola found it in the garage, on the floor, in front of the door to the garden and facing the other boxes, her boxes. It was smaller than the rest. Too light to contain the collection of *National Geographic*s and too heavy for a fixed wrench or a box of cocoa. She carried it to the living room and put it on the table next to her list. Stuck to the front, very neatly, was one of the labels she used to catalog things. His name was written on the first line, and she read it out loud.

Almost everything had gone bad. She could see from the bedroom that only the tomatoes and lemons were left in the garden. In the front yard, the impatiens, the Chinese lanterns, and the azaleas could no longer be saved. The mail was in the box beside the front gate, but no one brought it into the house. The yogurts had run out, and the crackers, the cans of tuna, the packets of noodles. There was a sign in the top drawer of the desk that said *The money is here*. There had been another, identical one in his night stand, *The money is here*, but that drawer had been opening for almost a week straight, for the man from the funeral home—who had seen to everything that needed seeing to without her having to leave the house—and for the delivery boy from the rotisserie every time he brought some chicken. So now the sign in that drawer was crossed out with thick marker. There were some bags of trash on the front porch of the house, because the garbagemen didn't jump the fence to get them. The cold would preserve the trash, Lola was counting on that. She had urgent things to resolve, and it had been hard to get her concentration back, to remember what was really important, to make some decisions. She had written a new item on her list. *He is dead.* She wondered if that one should go on a separate list. But the important thing was what needed to be remembered and what didn't, and in that sense, all the items were justified. Keeping his death in mind saved her some distress regarding the state of certain things in the house. If she concentrated on certain things, if she spent some hours of intense classification and labeling or sat for longer than advisable in front of the TV, she would raise her head a second to listen for his sounds, to locate him in the house, to figure out what it was he could be doing.

One night, sitting in front of the TV, she heard a noise coming from the bathroom. It sounded like pebbles against the windowpane. Hadn't she heard that sound before? For some reason she remembered the privet hedge that separated her yard from the woman's. She remembered the ditch. More sounds came, repeating insistently for some seconds, and Lola almost got distracted again, but then another presentiment reminded her of what was important. She felt it in her body, a physical warning that put her on the alert. She turned down the volume on the TV. With one hand on her knees and the other on the chair's backrest, she lifted her weight by leaning toward the center of the living room. Now she was standing. She went to the garage and turned on the light. The two large ceiling lamps illuminated the boxes. The car had remained outside after the last time he used it, and now almost everything was in boxes. She saw them all together now, as if she had never before taken the measure of her work. She thought about the furniture she had just walked past and understood that all the drawers must be practically empty. She looked at the workbench behind her that used to be cluttered with jars of nails, ropes, cables, and tools, and she discovered it had all already been taken care of as well. She knew when and how she had done it, but for a moment she was frightened by the thought that someone else might be packing things up. Then she remembered how there'd been other times she had planned to organize things in the garage, only to go out there and find she had already done it. And how she had opened the bathroom cabinet and been startled to see it empty, and also to find the garbage in the doorway, and the ruined garden. Her breathing grew agitated, but she focused on remaining calm. Atop the boxes she saw one that was smaller, a box that was clearly different. She would never cross the tape that way, without reinforcing the opening end to end so the cardboard wouldn't open if it held too much weight. She approached it. A label, the kind she herself used, bore his name. And then she also remembered that. She remembered he was dead, and that he had packed this box. And she also found another label, farther down, one in her own handwriting that said *Do not open*. But she couldn't remember if she'd opened it already or not, and if this was perhaps a warning. Maybe there was a lot more that she wasn't remembering. She would have to write other things on the list, additional things that she shouldn't forget. She went to the kitchen for her notebook and found it where she expected, and that was good. About to return to the garage, she stopped. There was a sign stuck to the refrigerator: a notebook page that said *My name is Lola, this is my house*. It was her handwriting. She heard a rough, ghostly sound, her body trembling, and she recognized it as her own breathing. She held on to the kitchen counter and went along it to the stool she used to wash dishes in front of the window. She saw the car parked outside and the tree in the front yard. She wondered if just a second ago she hadn't seen the tree trunk swelling up, if the boy wasn't crouched behind it, ready to enter the house as soon as she let her guard down. Faced with that danger, she realized she was still there, taking care of all the things, in charge of the house, the shopping, the garbage, in charge of everything there was in the world while he was sound asleep in the next room.

What was it that was important? She was hungry, but soon forgot her hunger. She went to the garage, returned to the living room, sat down in his armchair. She picked up two *National Geographic*s from the floor, wondered what they were doing there. She heard a knocking at the door: there was someone out there, and maybe they had knocked before. She held on to the magazines so they would remind her what she had been doing and went to open the door. It was the neighbor woman. Lola was shocked again at the sight of those deep gray circles under her eyes. The woman wanted to ask if she was all right. Lola needed a moment to think about how to reply, and then it was like going back all those days in the past. She remembered the boy. Remembered that the boy would spend whole afternoons with him. Remembered what had happened at the rotisserie, and that the boy had disappeared. And she also remembered the boxes and that she had wanted to die for years, and that she was still alive, alive even without him.

"Do you need anything?" asked the woman.

Lola had hunched over a little, bringing her hands to her chest, but immediately looked up.

"I'm sick," she said. "I'm going to die soon."

"I see," said the woman.

They were silent for a moment. Then the woman took a step toward the street and turned back toward Lola.

"Those boxes you offered me . . . Do you still have them?"

"Boxes . . ."

Lola thought about the boxes, about whether she had extra boxes—she didn't—about what would be the convenient thing to do at that moment. She thought that if the boxes were for the woman to move—which would be very convenient—she could empty some that were already packed and ask her to return them later. But the woman seemed to want them for something else, and if that was the case she would want to keep them, or donate them, or even burn them, but in no way would they be boxes Lola would ever see again.

"What do you need the boxes for?" asked Lola.

"I want to store my son's things."

"He doesn't live with you anymore?"

"Lola, my son is dead, I've told you that so many times."

Something loosened and expanded, and Lola could feel it inside, near her esophagus, like a pill stuck in her throat that finally dissolved. She thought about the cocoa powder, about the stool that had been left out in his garden, amid the dead leaves. Then she saw the *National Geographic*s dangling from her right hand and she wondered if he had messed the magazines up again, if once again she would be responsible for his negligence and disarray.

"They found him in the ditch," said the woman, and Lola wondered why this woman was looking at her that way. "You really didn't hear anything? Not even when the police came?"

If she took a step forward, Lola would have to step back, and then they would both be inside the house. It was a dangerous situation.

"Someone called the police to tell them my son had spent hours in that ditch, but by then it was too late."

Lola put her hand in her pocket and caressed the worn paper of her list. She had a clear intuition that she had added new items, but she couldn't remember what they were, and it seemed impolite to look just then.

"And I think it was you," said the woman.

Lola waited. She looked at the woman in suspicion. "What do you mean?"

"You saw my son in the ditch."

"Who are you?"

"You don't know who I am, but you can always remember the boxes."

Lola caressed the paper in her pocket; she really needed to read her list.

"I can't lend you boxes, I'm using them all." Lola wondered what could be in the boxes, and immediately she remembered. Then she remembered him: "My god, he's dead . . ."

"That's right, and I think you were the one who called the police."

This confused Lola again.

"I'm sorry, I don't understand what you're talking about."

Lola took out her list—she couldn't help it—opened it, and read it to herself. The list said:

Throw out broken things.

Wrap what is important.

Concentrate on death.

He is dead.

The woman took a step forward, Lola took one backward, and now they were in the house. In an instinctive reaction, Lola pushed her, and the woman stepped backward beyond the doorstep, almost tripping from the momentum that left her on the path, two stairs down. Lola closed the door, locked it, and waited. She waited a minute, attentive to the silence and the doorknob, and then she waited another minute. Nothing happened. Two minutes is a long time, her knees and ankles hurt, her back ached, but she waited. She steeled herself and looked out the peephole; the woman was gone. She found her pen and added at the end of her list:

The woman next door is dangerous.

Then she read the list again. There were many important things, and the first two items no longer qualified. She crossed them out. She wrote something else at the bottom. Now the list said:

Concentrate on death.

He is dead.

The woman next door is dangerous.

If you don't remember, wait.

A noise woke her up but she didn't open her eyes, and she told herself she'd done the right thing. Because this was no longer about the intruder in the front yard, or the banging on the fence. This sound was subtle and close by, inside the room. If she opened her eyes, she told herself, she might have to face something terrible. She focused on controlling her eyelids. She was ready for death, and what a relief it would be if this had only been death; she didn't want to suffer, didn't want anyone to hurt her, and again came the noise on the wooden floor, unmistakably human. Was it him? No, she told herself silently. He is dead. She opened her eyes. The boy was standing at the foot of the bed. She couldn't see his face, only his dark silhouette. She wanted to ask how he'd gotten in, but she realized she couldn't speak, and she wondered if it was because she was scared or because the boy had done something to her, something to keep her from talking or screaming. Slowly, clutching his arm, the boy sat down on the edge of the bed. Lola had to move her feet and draw up her legs to keep from touching him. She thought he looked thinner, more feeble. When he looked at her his face was completely dark, and she could discern no expression. Where was her husband every time the boy tried to scare her? Lola did nothing when the boy stood up and walked toward the kitchen. She followed him by the sounds he made. She heard him stumble as he walked; twice, he ran into the furniture. He opened the cupboard doors, one after another, until, after a final slam, everything was silent. Had he found the cocoa powder?

She could see the grain of the wood. She closed her eyes and opened them again. She was lying on the living room floor. What was she doing on the floor? She patted her apron pocket for her list, but it wasn't there. The side of her body that she was lying on hurt. She got up slowly, checking to be sure her legs worked properly. The usual aches were still there. She went toward the kitchen. There were garbage bags in the hallway, leaning against the empty shelves. She crossed the kitchen and went into the garage. There were more boxes than she remembered, and she thought maybe he had been packing things up behind her back. She put her hands in her pockets, and that's how she discovered the gauze around her fingers.

She took out her hands and looked at them. There was gauze wrapped around the index finger and thumb of her right hand and the entire wrist of her left. It was all stained with a dried red substance. She felt hungry and went back to the kitchen. A sign on the faucet said *Right to turn on, left to turn off*; another sign to one side said *Left*, and to the other side another sign said *Right*. The milk was out, on the stove, and the sign on the milk said *Keep in the refrigerator.* There was a list a little farther on, but it wasn't her list, the list of important things. This list said *You need to put the bag of milk into a bowl so the milk doesn't spill.* She wasn't sure she still wanted any milk, so she stopped reading and threw the list into the trash. Then she heard a rumbling sound behind her. Quiet but still perceptible to Lola, who was alert and knew her space. She heard it again, this time coming from the ceiling, and again, much closer, surrounding her entirely. It came and went like a rough, deep snore, like the breathing of a large animal inside the house. She looked at the ceiling and the walls; she peered out the window. Then she spoke aloud, reminded herself that she had already heard that sound and that it was delaying her more and more in what she had to do. She told herself she couldn't allow any more distractions. What was it she had to do?

All three mirrors in the house were broken, the shattered glass scattered on the floor, more glass sloppily swept along the wall. She was sure it had been the boy. That boy—*his* boy—had taken all the food in the cupboards and was breaking everything. Had he also taken the cocoa powder? She sat up in bed. Something smelled very bad, acidic and old. She put on her stockings and sandals. Then she heard him again: he was back in the house, stealing, breaking, eating. She got to her feet—furious, she couldn't take this anymore—and left the bedroom tying her dressing gown. She went to the front door. The sign on it said *Don't forget the keys*, so she grabbed them and left. She was surprised by the afternoon light; she had been sure it was morning, but she told herself that now she needed to focus on this new idea. She skirted the garbage, crossed through the weeds to her front gate, which was wide open, and went out to the sidewalk. She hesitated, looked down at her feet, her wet sandals, then started walking again to the woman's front door, where she rang the bell. Everything happened very fast. She had no pain, no respiratory complications, and when the woman answered, Lola wasn't at all sure she was doing the right thing.

"Hello," said Lola.

The woman stood looking at her. She was so skinny and pale, and it was so clear she was a sick woman, or a drug addict, that Lola grew worried about the consequences of what she had to tell her.

"Your son is stealing from me."

And she had such terrible circles under her eyes.

"He emptied my cupboards."

Something flashed in the depths of the woman's eyes, and her features hardened even more. She took in air, more air than such a slight woman could need, and she closed the door behind her—as if Lola had any intention of going into that house.

"Ma'am . . ."

"And it's not the first time he's done it."

"My son is dead."

Her voice sounded cold and metallic, like an answering machine, and Lola wondered how people could say such things with no compunction.

"Your son is living out behind my house, and he's breaking all my mirrors." Lola spoke in a firm, strong voice, and didn't regret doing so.

The woman took a step back and pressed her temples with her fists.

"I can't deal with you anymore. I just can't," said the woman.

Lola's hands went to her pockets; she knew there was something important there but she couldn't remember what.

"You have to calm down," said Lola.

The woman nodded. She breathed and lowered her fists.

"Lola," said the woman.

How did this woman know her name?

"Lola, my son is dead. And you are sick." She took

another, unsteady step backward, and Lola thought she looked drunk, or like she had lost control of her nerves. "You are sick, understand? And you ring my doorbell . . ." Her eyes filled with tears. "All the time."

The woman pressed the bell of her own house twice, and the noise was annoying as it rang out over their heads.

"All the time, you ring and ring," she pressed it again so hard that her finger bent back on the button, and still harder, violently. "To tell me that my son is alive out behind your house." Her voice rose abruptly. "My son, the son I buried with my own hands because you are a stupid old woman who didn't call the police in time."

She pushed Lola backward and slammed the door. Lola heard her crying inside. Heard her cry out as she walked away. Another loud slam at the back of the house. Lola stood looking at her sandals. They were so wet they left prints on the concrete. She took a few steps to be sure, then looked at the sky and realized Dr. Petterson's show must be about to start, but then she remembered her reason for coming here and she walked up the two steps and rang the bell. She waited. She focused her attention and heard some noises in the depths of the house. She looked back down at her sandals, which were wet, and then she remembered again that Dr. Petterson's show was about to start, and she walked down the steps slowly, very slowly, calculating the strategy that would get her back to her house as quickly as possible without agitating her breathing in her lungs.

But Lola remembered the incident at the supermarket perfectly. She'd been looking for a new product in the canned food aisle. It was hot because the employees of that store didn't know how to work the air conditioner well. She remembers prices; ten pesos and ninety cents, for example, was the cost of the can of tuna she was holding in her hand when she felt an uncontrollable need to urinate pressing on her bladder. That was when she noticed another woman a little farther down, near the dairy section, concentrated on the yogurt selection. She was around forty years old and overly stout, so much so that Lola couldn't help thinking about just what kind of husband a woman like that could get, and also that, if she had looked that way at that age, she would have found a way to lose a little weight. She felt pressure in her bladder again, this time a bit more intense than usual, and Lola understood it was no longer a containable need but an emergency. Another throb of pressure startled her and she dropped the can of tuna, which hit the floor. She saw the woman turn toward her. She was afraid a little pee had escaped; she was disgusted, and swallowed hard. These things didn't happen to her, so as she felt the wetness she told herself it was just a few drops, no one would notice with the skirt she was wearing. It was precisely then that she saw him; he was sitting in the other woman's shopping cart, looking at Lola. She didn't recognize him at first—for a second he was just a normal boy, a child of around two or three years old sitting in the shopping cart seat. Until she saw his dark, shining eyes gazing at her, his little hands, small but so strong, grasping the metal bar, and she felt certain that this was her son. The hot wetness of the urine spread through her underpants. She took two clumsy steps backward and saw the other woman coming toward her. And still another thing happened, something she couldn't tell anyone, not the hospital doctor or her husband. Something she still remembers, because she has forgotten nothing about that day. It wasn't a trick of mirrors. That other woman was Lola, thirty-five years ago. It was a terrifying certainty. Fat and unkempt, she watched herself approach with identical repulsion.

Dr. Petterson was still there, looking at her from the TV and showing her a can of food. She was standing, holding on to the table with one hand. With the other she lowered the zipper on her skirt to let it fall, but it was stuck to her body and she had to push it down to get it off. The boy was sitting in her husband's armchair. Only then did she see him, and they looked at each other. Lola didn't know what the boy was thinking, or what she herself thought about the boy. All she knew was that she was very hungry, and that her twenty-four peaches-and-cream yogurts were no longer in the fridge. Then she remembered the cocoa powder, and she saw herself eating it in the darkened kitchen, with a spoon. Had it been her, all this time? Was it possible? Did he know? Where was he? She heard a deep rumbling sound. So deep that the floor trembled under her body. It came again, dark and heavy inside her. It was her breath rising from the depths, a great prehistoric monster pummeling her painfully from the center of her body. And yet, this was what she had longed for, she told herself intuitively. Leaning against the wall, she slid down to the floor. She focused on the pain. Because if this was death, the pain was the final blow she needed in order to die. This was the only thing she had wanted, it was what she had wished for during so many years, though it had come only for him. To be done. Her heart sped up, it pounded in her chest and further roused the monster; the voices went silent, she let herself go, sink down and disappear, leave the discomfort behind. She saw a silent image. The memory of a warm afternoon at her grandparents' country house, holding the skirt of her blue dress filled with wildflowers. And another image, the first time he had cooked for her, the table set, the sweet perfume of meat with plums. Then Lola returned to her body, and her body returned her pain. She felt the cutting air rise and fall in her flesh. In her lungs, a stabbing pain came with her final revelation: she wasn't ever going to die, because to die she would have to remember his name, because his name was also her son's, the name that was on the box, a few feet away. But the abyss had opened up, and words and things were moving away at full speed, with the light, now very far from her body.

Two

Square

Feet

My mother-in-law wants me to buy aspirin. She gives me two ten-peso bills and tells me how to get to the nearest pharmacy.

"Are you sure you don't mind going?"

I shake my head and walk toward the door. I try not to think about the story she's just told me, but the apartment is small and I have to dodge so many pieces of furniture, so many shelves and cabinets full of knickknacks, that it's hard to think about anything else. I leave the apartment and enter the dark hallway. I don't turn on the lights; I'd rather let the light come of its own accord when the elevator doors open up and illuminate me.

My mother-in-law put up a Christmas tree over the fireplace. It's a gas fireplace with artificial rocks, and she insists on bringing it along every time she moves to a new apartment. The Christmas tree is pint-sized, skinny, and a light, artificial green. It has round red ornaments, two gold garlands, and six Santa Claus figures dangling from the branches like a club of hanged men. I pause to look at it several times a day, or else I picture it while I'm doing other things. I think about how my mother used to buy garlands that were much fluffier and softer, and about how the Santa Clauses' eyes are not painted exactly over the ocular depressions where they should be.

When I reach the pharmacy she directed me to, I see that it's closed. It is ten fifteen p.m., so I'll have to find an all-night pharmacy. I don't know the neighborhood and I don't want to call Mariano, so I make a guess based on the traffic as to where the nearest major street is, and I walk that way. I have to get used to this city again.

Before Mariano and I left for Spain, we handed over the apartment we'd been renting and boxed up the things we weren't taking with us. My mother brought us boxes from work, forty-seven boxes for Mendoza wine that we assembled as we needed them. The two times Mariano left my mother and me alone, she asked me again about the real reason we were going, but I couldn't answer either time. A moving van took everything to a storage unit. I remember all this because I'm almost positive that in the box that says *Bathroom* there's a blister pack of aspirin. But now that we're back in Buenos Aires, we still haven't gone to get those boxes. We have to find a new apartment first, and before that, we have to save back some of the money we lost.

A little while ago my mother-in-law told me that horrible story, but she told it proudly and said that someone should write it. It took place before her divorce, before she sold the house and helped with the money for Spain. After she told it her blood pressure dropped and she got a terrible headache, and she sent me out to buy aspirin. She thinks I miss my mother, and she can't understand why I don't want to call her.

I see a pharmacy a block farther, on the avenue, and I wait for the light so I can cross. This one is closed, too, but it has a list of on-duty pharmacies. If I have my bearings right, there's one on the other side of Santa Fe, past the tracks of the Carranza station. It's about four blocks farther, and I've already gone pretty far. I think it would be good if Mariano came home and asked his mother where I was, so she would have to explain herself and tell him she sent me out to buy aspirin at ten thirty at night in an unfamiliar neighborhood. Then I wonder why that would be a good thing.

The first thing my mother-in-law told me was that she was standing in the middle of the dining room of her house. Her husband was at work but would be home soon. Her four sons were out, too, one working with their father, the others in school. She had fought with her husband again the night before, and she'd asked him for a divorce. The house was big, and she had lost control of it. The cleaning lady was in charge of the house now, and she herself could no longer say what was kept in the closets or what went into the cupboards. When they sat around the table, her sons would watch her eat and laugh. If there was chicken, she gnawed anxiously at the bones; if there was dessert, she served herself a double portion; she drank water with her mouth full. *It's just that I'm very alone*, she'd think to herself, *and my sons only believe in their father.*

I turn down the first street to cross but it's closed off, a dead end, and the same thing happens the next block down. I look around for someone to ask, and I find a woman who peers at me suspiciously. She says that two blocks down I can cross to the other side of Santa Fe through the subway tunnels.

So, that day, my mother-in-law was standing in the middle of the dining room, and she looked down at her hands and decided on her next move. She grabbed her coat and purse, left the house, and took a taxi to Calle Libertad. It was pouring down rain, but she felt that if she didn't do what she had to do right then, she never would. When she got out of the taxi the water was up to her ankles, and her sandals got soaked. She rang the bell at a shop that bought and sold gold. She saw the salesman walk toward her between the illuminated display cases. I suppose he opened the door and looked her up and down, sorry that someone so sodden was going to enter his shop. Inside, the air-conditioning was on very high and blew right on the back of her neck.

"I want to sell this ring," she said. She thought it would be hard to take off because she had gained a lot of weight, but she was soaked from the rain and the ring slid off easily.

The man placed it on a small electronic scale.

"I can give you thirty dollars for it."

It took her a few seconds to answer. Then she said:

"It's my wedding ring."

And the man said:

"That's what it's worth."

Now I go down into the subway and take the tunnel to cross the avenue. I see a bifurcation sign and then I recognize the place; I remember I've been here before. To the right and down two more flights of stairs is the subway stop; to the left is the exit. Maybe because I think there might be a pharmacy in the subway, or because I want to remember the station a little more, I go to the right. I waste time because it helps me move forward; for a month and a half now I've had absolutely nothing to do. So I go toward the station. I have a card on me that still works, and a train is arriving. The wheels give a little shriek and the doors open in unison. There aren't many people on the platform because service ends at eleven. Someone leans out from the first car, maybe a security guard who's wondering whether I'm going to get on or not. When the train moves off I sit down on one of the empty benches. The station falls into silence, and then something moves a little beyond the bench. It's an old man, a beggar, sitting on the floor, with legs that end in stumps just above his knees. He's looking at the shampoo ad that's on the other side of the tracks.

My mother-in-law accepted the money, she told me, and she left the shop stroking her ring finger. It was no longer raining outside but the water still reached the storefronts, and her wet sandals wounded her feet. A few days later she would exchange the dollars in her pockets for a pair of sandals that she could never bring herself to wear, and even so, she would remain married for twenty-six months longer. She told me this in the dining room while she painted her nails. She said she didn't need the money she'd given us for Spain, and we could pay her back whenever we wanted. She said she missed her sons a lot, but she knew they were busy with their own lives, and she didn't want to be a burden on them by calling every time she'd really like to call. I thought I had to listen to her, that it was my obligation because I was living in her house, and because I felt guilty she no longer had her thirty-dollar ring. Because she insisted on cooking for us, on ironing our clothes every time we washed them, because she had been so good to me right from the start. She also said she asked the neighbor in apartment C for the Sunday classifieds, and she checked to see if she could find a better place to move into, because she didn't think this one had enough light either. I listened to her because I didn't have anything else to do, and I looked at her because she was sitting in front of the Christmas tree. And finally she said that she loved chatting with me, just like this, like two girlfriends. That when she was little, in the kitchen of her childhood home, they'd talked about everything, and that she wishes her mother was still with her. She was quiet for a while so I tried to open my magazine again, but then she said:

"When I ask God for something I do it like this:

'God, do the best you can,'" and she gave a long sigh. "Really, I don't ask for anything specific. I've listened to people enough to know they don't always ask for what's best for them."

And then she said her head really hurt, that she felt dizzy, and she asked if I would mind going for some aspirin.

Another train pulls away from the platform. The old man looks at me and says:

"You're not taking one either?"

"I need my boxes," I say, because suddenly I remember them again and that's how I realize what it is I want, why I am still sitting on this bench.

But my mother-in-law said something else. Something very silly that I just couldn't get out of my head. She said that after she left the store with her thirty dollars, she couldn't go home. She had money for a taxi, she knew her address, she didn't have anything else to do, but she simply couldn't do it. She walked to the bus stop on the corner and sat down on the metal bench, and there she stayed. She looked at the people. She couldn't, didn't want to think about anything or make any decisions.

All she could do was look and breathe because her body did that automatically. An indefinite period of time passed cyclically, the bus came and went, the stop emptied and filled up again. The waiting people were always holding something. They carried their things in bags, in purses, under an arm, hanging from their hands, or rested them on the ground between their feet. They were there to care for their things, and in exchange those things sustained them.

The old man climbs up onto my bench. I can't figure out how he does it, and I'm startled that he can move so quickly. He smells like garbage, but he's friendly. He takes a city guide from his bag.

"You want your boxes," he says, and he opens the guide toward me, "but you don't know how to get there . . ."

Though it's an old guide, I recognize the city's subway stations on the map. From Retiro to Constitución, and from downtown to Chacarita.

My mother-in-law said she remembers everything; she remembers so clearly she could describe every one of those things the people were carrying. But her own hands were empty. And she wasn't going anywhere. She said she was sitting on two square feet, that's what she said. I didn't understand at first. It's hard to imagine my mother-in-law saying something like that, though it is what she said: that she was sitting on two square feet, and that was all the space she took up in the world.

The old man is waiting for me. He looks down for a second and I see he has a pair of eyes drawn on his eyelids, just like the Santa Clauses on the Christmas tree. I think I should stand up, that once I'm at the storage unit I'll recognize the box I need. But I can't do it. I can't even move. If I stand up I'll have to see how much room my body really occupies. And if I look at the map—the old man holds it out a little closer to me, in case that will help—I'll find that, in the whole city, there is no place I can point to.

An

Unlucky

Man

The day I turned eight, my sister—who absolutely always had to be the center of attention—swallowed an entire cup of bleach. Abi was three. First she smiled, maybe in disgust; then her face crumpled in a frightened grimace of pain. When Mom saw the empty cup hanging from Abi's hand, she turned as white as my sister.

"Abi-my-god," was all Mom said. "Abi-my-god," and it took her a few more seconds before she sprang into action.

She shook Abi by the shoulders, but my sister didn't respond. She yelled, but Abi still didn't react. Mom ran to the phone and called Dad, and when she came running back Abi was still standing there, the cup just dangling from her hand. Mom grabbed the cup and threw it into the sink. She opened the fridge, took out the milk, and poured a glass. She stood looking at the glass, then looked at Abi, then back at the glass, and finally dropped the glass into the sink as well. Dad worked very close by and got home quickly, but Mom still had time to do the whole show with the glass of milk again before he pulled up in the car and started honking the horn and yelling.

Mom lit out of the house like lightning, with Abi clutched to her chest. The front door, the gate, and the car doors were all flung open. There was more horn honking, and Mom, who was already sitting in the car, started to cry. Dad had to shout at me twice before I understood that I was the one who was supposed to close up.

We drove the first ten blocks in less time than it had taken me to close the car door and fasten my seat belt. But when we got to the main avenue, the traffic was prac-

tically at a standstill. Dad honked the horn and shouted
out the window, "We have to get to the hospital! We have
to get to the hospital!" The cars around us maneuvered
and miraculously let us pass, but a couple cars ahead we
had to start the whole operation over again. Dad braked,
stopped honking, and began to pound his head against
the steering wheel. I had never seen him do such a thing.
There was a moment of silence, and then he sat up and
looked at me in the rearview mirror. He turned around
and said to me:

"Take off your underpants."

I was wearing my school uniform. All my underwear
was white, but I wasn't exactly thinking about that just
then, and I couldn't understand Dad's request. I pressed
my hands into the seat to support myself better. I looked
at Mom and she shouted:

"Take off your damned underpants!"

I took them off. Dad grabbed them out of my hands.
He rolled down the window, went back to honking the
horn, and started waving my underpants out the window. He raised them high while he yelled and kept honking, and it seemed like everyone on the avenue turned

around to look at them. My underpants were small, but they were also very white. An ambulance a block behind us turned on its siren, caught up with us quickly, and started clearing a path. Dad kept waving the underpants until we reached the hospital.

He parked the car by the ambulances and they jumped out. Without waiting, Mom took Abi and ran straight into the hospital. I wasn't sure whether I should get out or not: I didn't have any underpants on, and I looked around to see where Dad had left them, but they weren't on the seat or in his hand, which was already slamming his car door behind him.

"Come on, come on," said Dad.

He opened my door and helped me out, then locked the car. He gave my shoulder a few pats as we walked into the emergency room. Mom came out of a doorway at the back and signaled to us. I was relieved to see she was talking again, giving explanations to the nurses.

"Stay here," said Dad, and he pointed to some orange chairs on the other side of the main waiting area.

I sat. Dad went into the consulting room with Mom

and I waited for a while. I don't know how long, but it felt long. I pressed my knees together tightly and thought about everything that had happened so quickly, and about the possibility that any of the kids from school had seen the whole display with my underpants. When I sat up straight, my jumper rode up and my bare bottom touched part of the plastic seat. Sometimes the nurse came in or out of the consulting room and I could hear my parents arguing. At one point I craned my neck and caught a glimpse of Abi squirming restlessly on one of the cots, and I knew that, at least today, she wasn't going to die. And I still had to wait.

Then a man came and sat down next to me. I don't know where he came from; I hadn't noticed him before.

"How's it going?" he asked.

I thought about saying "Very well," which is what Mom always said if someone asked her that, even if she'd just told me and Abi that we were driving her insane.

"Okay," I said.

"Are you waiting for someone?"

I thought about it. I wasn't *really* waiting for anyone; at least, it wasn't what I *wanted* to be doing right then. So I shook my head, and he said:

"Why are you sitting in the waiting room, then?"

I understood it was a great contradiction. He opened a small bag he had on his lap and rummaged around in it, unhurried. Then he took a pink slip of paper from his wallet.

"Here it is. I knew I had it somewhere."

The paper was printed with the number 92.

"It's good for an ice cream cone. My treat," he said.

I told him no. You shouldn't accept things from strangers.

"But it's free, I won it."

"No." I looked straight ahead and we sat in silence.

"Suit yourself," he said, without getting angry.

He took a magazine from his bag and started to fill in a crossword puzzle. The door to the consulting room opened again and I heard Dad say, "I will not condone such nonsense." I remember because that's Dad's clincher for ending almost any argument, but the man didn't seem to hear it.

"It's my birthday," I said.

It's my birthday, I repeated to myself. What should I do?

The man held the pen to mark a box on the puzzle and looked at me in surprise. I nodded without looking at him, aware that I had his attention again.

"But . . ." he said, and he closed the magazine. "Sometimes I just don't understand women. If it's your birthday, what are you doing in a hospital waiting room?"

He was an observant man. I straightened up again in my seat and I saw that, even then, I only came up to his shoulders. He smiled and I smoothed my hair. And then I said:

"I'm not wearing any underpants."

I don't know why I said it. It's just that it was my birthday and I wasn't wearing underpants, and I couldn't stop thinking about those circumstances. He was still looking at me. Maybe he was startled or offended, and I understood that, though it hadn't been my intention, there was something vulgar about what I had just said.

"But it's your birthday," he said.

I nodded.

"It's not fair. A person can't just go around without underpants when it's their birthday."

"I know," I said emphatically, because now I understood just how Abi's whole display was a personal affront to me.

He sat for a moment without saying anything. Then he glanced toward the big windows that looked out onto the parking lot.

"I know where to get you some underpants," he said.

"Where?"

"Problem solved." He stowed his things and stood up.

I hesitated. Precisely because I wasn't wearing underpants, but also because I didn't know if he was telling the truth. He looked toward the front desk and waved one hand at the attendants.

"We'll be right back," he said, and pointed to me. "It's her birthday." And then I thought, *Oh please dear Jesus, don't let him say anything about my underpants*, but he didn't: he opened the door and winked at me, and then I knew I could trust him.

We went out to the parking lot. Standing, I came up

to just above his waist. Dad's car was still next to the ambulances, and a policeman was circling it, annoyed. I kept looking over at the policeman, and he watched us walk away. The breeze wrapped around my legs and rose, making a tent out of my uniform skirt. I had to hold it down while I walked, keeping my legs awkwardly close together.

He turned around to see if I was following him, and he saw me fighting with my jumper.

"We'd better stick close to the wall."

"I want to know where we're going."

"Don't get persnickety with me now, darling."

We crossed the avenue and went into a shopping center. It was an uninviting place, and I was pretty sure Mom didn't go there. We walked to the back where there was a big clothing store, a truly huge one that I don't think Mom had ever been to, either. Before we went in he said, "Don't get lost," and gave me his hand, which was cold and very soft. He waved to the cashiers the same way he'd waved to the desk attendants when we left the hospital, but I didn't see anyone respond. We walked down the aisles. In addition to dresses, pants, and shirts, there were work clothes: hard hats, yellow overalls like the ones trash collectors wear, smocks for cleaning ladies, plastic boots, and even some tools. I wondered if he bought his clothes there and if he would use any of those things in his job, and then I also wondered what his name was.

"Here we are," he said.

We were surrounded by tables of underwear for men and women. If I reached out my hand I could touch a large bin full of giant underpants, bigger than any I'd seen before, and they were only three pesos each. With one of those pairs of underpants, they could have made three for someone my size.

"Not those," he said. "Here." And he led me a little farther to a section with smaller sizes.

"Just look at all the underpants they have . . . Which pair shall you choose, my lady?"

I looked around. Almost all of them were white or pink. I pointed to a white pair, one of the few that didn't have a bow on them.

"These," I said. "But I can't pay for them."

He came a bit closer and said into my ear:

"That doesn't matter."

"Are you the owner?"

"No. It's your birthday."

I smiled.

"But we have to find better ones. We need to be sure."

"Okay, darling," I ventured.

"Don't say 'darling,'" he said, "or I'll get persnickety." And he imitated me holding down my skirt in the parking lot.

He made me laugh. When he finished clowning around he held out two closed fists in front of me, and he stayed just like that until I understood; I touched the right one. He opened it: empty.

"You can still choose the other one."

I touched the other one. It took me a moment to realize it was a pair of underpants, because I had never seen black ones before. And they were for girls because they had white hearts on them, so small they looked like dots, and Hello Kitty's face was on the front, right where there was usually that bow Mom and I don't like at all.

"You'll have to try them on," he said.

I held the underpants to my chest. He gave me his hand again and we went toward the changing rooms, which looked empty. We peered inside. He said he didn't know if he could go in with me, because they were for women only. He said I would have to go alone. It was logical because, unless it's someone you know very well, it's not good for people to see you in your underpants. But I was afraid of going into the dressing room alone. Or something worse: coming out and finding no one there.

"What's your name?" I asked.

"I can't tell you that."

"Why not?

He knelt down. Then he was almost my height, or maybe I was a couple inches taller.

"Because I'm cursed."

"Cursed? What's cursed?"

"A woman who hates me said that the next time I say my name, I'm going to die."

An Unlucky Man

I thought it might be another joke, but he said it very seriously.

"You could write it down for me."

"Write it down?"

"If you wrote it you wouldn't say it, you'd be writing it. And if I know your name, I can call for you and I won't be so scared to go into the dressing room alone."

"But we can't be sure. What if this woman thinks writing my name is the same as saying it? What if for her, saying it means informing someone else, letting my name out into the world in any way?"

"But how would she know?"

"People don't trust me, and I'm the unluckiest man in the world."

"I don't believe you, there's no way to know that."

"I know what I'm talking about."

Together, we looked at the underpants in my hands. I thought that my parents might be finished by now.

"But it's my birthday," I said.

And maybe I did it on purpose. At the time I felt like I did: my eyes filled with tears. Then he hugged me. It was a very fast movement; he crossed his arms behind my back and squeezed me so tight my face pressed into his chest. Then he let me go, took out his magazine and pen, and wrote something on the right edge of the cover. Then he tore it off and folded it three times before handing it to me.

"Don't read it," he said, and he stood up and pushed me gently toward the dressing room.

I passed four empty cubicles. Before gathering my courage and entering the fifth, I put the paper into my jumper pocket and turned to look at him, and we smiled at each other.

I tried on the underpants. They were perfect. I lifted up my skirt so I could see just how good they looked. They were so, so very perfect. They fit incredibly well, and because they were black, Dad would never ask me for them so he could wave them out the window behind the ambulance. And even if he did, I wouldn't be so embarrassed if my classmates saw. "Just look at the underpants that girl has," they'd all think. "Now, those are some perfect underpants."

I realized I couldn't take them off now. And I realized something else: they didn't have a security tag. They had a little mark where the tag would usually go, but there was no alarm. I stood a moment longer looking at myself in the mirror, and then I couldn't stand it anymore and I took out the little paper, opened it, and read it.

I came out of the dressing room and he wasn't where I had left him, but just a little farther away, next to the bathing suits. He looked at me, and when he saw I wasn't carrying the underpants he winked, and I was the one who took his hand. This time he clasped me tighter and I was fine with that; together, we walked toward the exit.

I trusted that he knew what he was doing, that a cursed man who had the world's worst luck knew how to do these things. We passed the line of registers at the main entrance. One of the security guards glanced at us and adjusted his belt. He would surely think my nameless man was my dad, and I felt proud.

We passed the sensors at the exit and went into the mall, and we kept walking in silence all the way back to the avenue. That was when I saw Abi, alone, in the middle of the hospital parking lot. And I saw Mom, on our side of the street, looking around frantically. Dad was also coming toward us from the parking lot. He was following fast behind the policeman who'd been looking at our car before, and who was now pointing at us. Everything happened very quickly. Dad saw us, yelled my name, and a few seconds later that policeman and two others who came out of nowhere were already on top of us. The unlucky man let go of me, but my hand hung there reaching out toward him for a few seconds. They surrounded him and shoved him roughly. They asked what he was doing, they asked his name, but he didn't answer. Mom hugged me and checked me over from head to toe. She had my white underpants dangling from her right hand. Then, patting me all over, she noticed I was wearing a different pair. She lifted my skirt in a single movement: it was such a rude and vulgar thing to do, right there in front of everyone, that I jerked away and had to take a few steps backward to keep from falling down. The unlucky man looked at me and I looked at him. When Mom saw the black underpants she screamed, "Son of a bitch, son of a bitch," and Dad lunged at him and tried to punch him. The cops moved to separate them.

I fished for the paper in my pocket, put it in my mouth, and as I swallowed it I repeated his name in silence, several times, so I would never forget it.

Out

Three flashes of lightning illuminate the night, and I catch a glimpse of dirty terraces and dividing walls. The rain hasn't started yet. The sliding glass door of the balcony across from us opens, and a woman in pajamas comes outside to bring in the clothes from the line. I see all this as I'm sitting at the dining table across from my husband, after a long silence. His hands encircle the cup of tea, now cold, and his red eyes are still gazing at me resolutely. He's waiting for me to be the one to say what must be said. And because I feel like he knows what it is I have to say, I can no longer say it. His blanket is balled up at the foot of the sofa, and the coffee table holds two empty mugs and an ashtray full of butts and used tissues. *I have to say it,* I tell myself, because it's part of the punishment I now have coming. I adjust the towel wrapped around my wet hair and tighten the knot of my robe. *I have to say it,* I repeat to myself, but it's an impossible command. And then something happens, something in my muscles that is difficult to explain. It happens step-by-step without my ever understanding exactly what it is: I simply push the chair back and stand up. I take two sideways steps away. *I have to say something,* I think, while my body takes two more steps and I lean against the china cabinet, my hands fumbling over the wood, holding myself up. I catch sight of the front door, and, since I know he is still looking at me, I take pains to avoid his eyes. I breathe, I concentrate. I take a step to the side, moving a little farther away. He says nothing, and I venture another step. My slippers are close by, and without letting go of the wooden cabinet, I reach out my feet to pull them toward me and put them on. My movements are slow, gradual.

Out

I let go of the cabinet, step a little farther away, as far as the rug, take a deep breath, and then, in only three long strides, I cross the living room, leave the apartment, and close the door behind me. My labored breathing echoes in the building's darkened hallway. I stand for a moment with my ear pressed to the door, trying to hear sounds from inside—his chair when he stands up or his footsteps coming toward me—but everything is completely silent. *I don't have keys,* I tell myself, and I'm not sure whether that worries me. *I am naked under my robe.* I'm aware of the problem, of the whole problem, but somehow my state, this extraordinary state of alertness, frees me from any kind of judgment. The fluorescent lights flicker on and the hallway turns slightly green. I go to the elevator and call it, and it comes immediately. The doors open and a man peers out without taking his hand from the buttons. He invites me in with a friendly gesture. When the doors close, I smell an intense lavender scent, as if they've just cleaned, and the light, warm now and very near our heads, relieves and comforts me.

"Do you know what time it is, miss?"

His deep voice confuses me, and it's hard to tell if his words are a question or a reproach. He's a very short man who only comes up to my shoulders, but he's older than me. He seems like a janitor or a hired plumber or electrician, though I know both the building's janitors and I've never seen this man before. He has almost no hair. His threadbare coveralls are open, and the clean, ironed shirt beneath makes him look crisp, or professional. He shakes his head, maybe to himself.

"My wife is going to kill me," he says.

I don't ask; I am not interested in knowing. I'm comfortable in his company going down, but I don't feel like listening. My arms hang loose and heavy at my sides, and I realize I'm relaxed, that leaving the apartment is doing me good.

"I don't even want to tell you," says the man, and he shakes his head again.

"I appreciate it," I say. I smile so he doesn't take it the wrong way.

"I don't even . . ."

We take our leave in the foyer with a nod.

Out

"Best of luck to you," he says.

"Thanks."

The man walks off toward the parking garage and I go out the front door. It's night, but I couldn't say exactly what time. I walk to the corner to see how much movement there is on Avenida Corrientes, and everything looks asleep. At the stoplight I take the towel from my head and drape it over my arm, and I run my fingers back through my hair. The days this week have been humid and hot, but now a pleasant breeze wafts from Chacarita, fresh and perfumed, and I walk in that direction. I think about my sister, about what my sister does, and I wish I could tell someone about it. People are very interested in what my sister does, and on occasion I like to talk about things that interest people. Then something happens that in a way I am expecting. Maybe because a second before hearing the horn I'd already thought about him, about the man in the elevator, and so I'm not troubled by his car pulling up or by his smile, and I think, *I can tell him about my sister.*

"Can I give you a ride somewhere?"

"You could," I say, "but the night is too nice to get into a car."

He nods; my observation seems to change his plans somehow. He stops the car and I approach.

"I'm headed home because my wife is going to kill me, and for that to happen I need to be there."

I nod.

"It's a joke," he says.

"Yeah, of course," I say, and smile.

He smiles, too, and I like his smile.

"But we could roll the windows down, all the windows, and drive the car nice and slow."

"Do you think we'd bother anyone, going so slow?"

He looks both ways down the avenue. He has hair on the nape of his neck, a little reddish fuzz.

"No, there's almost no one out. We could do it, no problem."

"Okay," I say.

I get in and settle into the passenger seat. He rolls down the windows and opens the sunroof. The car is old but comfortable, and it smells of lavender.

"Why is your wife going to kill you?" I ask, because

before I tell someone about my sister, I ask them a question first.

He puts the car in first and concentrates for a moment on the clutch and the accelerator, moving the car slowly until it reaches a comfortable speed. He looks at me and I nod in approval.

"Today is our anniversary, and I was supposed to pick her up at eight so we could go out to eat. But there was a problem with the roof of the building. Did you hear?"

The air moves along my arms and over my neck, neither cold nor hot. *Perfect,* I think, *this is all I needed.*

"Are you a new maintenance man in the building?"

"Well, depends what you count as 'new' . . . I've been at the building for six months now, miss."

"And are you a roofer as well?"

"I'm an escapist, really."

We're driving very close to the sidewalk, almost on the heels of a woman who's carrying an empty supermarket bag and walking quickly; she looks at us sideways.

"An escapist?"

"I fix fire escapes."

"Are you sure that's what an escapist does?"

"I can assure you it is."

The woman on the sidewalk looks at us in annoyance and slows down so we have to pass her.

"Anyway, now it's too late to go out to eat, and she must have spent hours waiting for me. Restaurants will all be closing by now."

"Did you call her to let her know you'd be late?"

He shakes his head, aware of his mistake.

"You don't want to give her a call?"

"No, I really don't think it's a good idea."

"Well then, there's not much you can do. You can't make any decisions until you get there and see how she is."

"That's what I think, too."

We look straight ahead. The night is still, and I'm not sleepy at all.

"I'm going to my sister's house."

"I thought your sister lived in the same building."

"She works in the building, her studio is two floors

above my place. But she lives somewhere else. Do you know her? Do you know what my sister does?"

"Excuse me, would you mind if I stop for a moment? I could really use a smoke."

He stops the car in front of a kiosk, turns the engine off, and gets out. *Everything is going great so far,* I think to myself. *I feel so good right now.* There seems to be something special in all of this, but what it is escapes me. *What sort of something?* I wonder. I have to know what it is that's working, so I can retain it and replicate it, so I'll be able to return to this state when I need to.

"Miss!"

The escapist is waving at me from the kiosk. I toss the towel in the backseat and get out.

"Neither of us has change," says the escapist, indicating the kiosk man.

They wait for me. I check the pocket of my robe for change.

"Are you okay?" asks the kiosk man.

Still focused as I am on my pockets, it takes me a moment to realize the question is directed at me.

"Your hair is wet," he says, pointing at me in surprise, "like you just got out of the shower." He looks at my robe, too, but says nothing about that. "Just say you're okay and we'll go back to the matter of change."

"I'm okay," I say, "but I don't have any change either."

The man nods, dubious, then crouches behind the counter. We hear him talking to himself, saying that somewhere in all these boxes there are always a few extra coins. The escapist looks at my hair. He is frowning, and for a moment I'm afraid something is breaking irreparably, some piece of this well-being.

"You know"—the kiosk man appears again—"I have a hair dryer in the back. If you want . . ."

I look at the escapist, alert to his reaction. I don't want to, I don't want to dry my hair, but nor do I want to refuse anything to anyone.

"We're working on that," says the escapist, pointing toward the car. "See? We're driving with the windows down, in first gear, and it's really hot. Soon her hair will be dry as a bone."

The man looks at the car. He has some coins in his

hand that he squeezes and jingles a couple of times before looking back at us and handing them to the escapist.

"Thanks," I say as we leave.

My demeanor doesn't seem to convince the kiosk
man, and though he walks off toward the coolers, he
still turns back a couple of times to look at us. Outside,
the escapist offers me a cigarette, but I tell him I've quit
smoking and I lean against the car, willing to wait. He
lights one and exhales the smoke upward, the way my
sister does. I think it's a good sign, and that once we're
moving again we can get back whatever it was that we
lost in the kiosk.

"Let's buy something," I tell him suddenly, "for your
wife. Something she likes and that will prove to her you
didn't mean to be late."

"Didn't mean to?"

"Flowers, or something sweet. Look, there's a service station over on the other corner. Shall we walk?"

He nods and locks the car. The windows are still
open, just as we had agreed when we started on this
outing. *That's very good*, I tell myself. And we walk
toward the corner. Our first steps are sloppy. He walks

close to the curb, with no rhythm, and he trips over his feet a few times, surprised by his own clumsiness. *He can't get in step*, I think, *I have to be patient.* I stop looking so as not to make him uncomfortable. I look at the sky, the streetlight; I turn around to see how far we are from the car. I move a little closer, trying to recover a communication distance. I walk a little more slowly to see if that helps, but then he just gets farther ahead, until he stops. Annoyed, he turns toward me and waits. When we're back together we coincide for a couple of steps, but soon we are out of sync once again. Then I'm the one who stops.

"It's not working," I say.

He takes a few more steps, circling me disconcertedly, looking at our feet.

"Let's go back," he says. "We can still keep going in the car."

A subway train passes underground, the sidewalk shakes, and a wave of hot air rises from the grated openings. I shake my head. A few meters back, the kiosk man comes out and looks at us. *This is no longer the right way*, I think, *and everything was going so well.* The escapist laughs, sad. My body contracts, and I feel my hands and the back of my neck grow rigid.

"This is not a game," I say.

"Come again?"

"This is very serious."

He doesn't move, and his smile disappears. He says:

"I'm sorry, but I'm not sure I really understand what's happening anymore."

We lost it, I think, *it's gone*. He stands looking at me, but his eyes have a shine to them; there's a second when the escapist's eyes look at me and seem to understand.

"Do you want to tell me about your sister?"

I shake my head.

"You want me to take you to the building?"

"It's only eight blocks, I'd better walk it alone. You call your wife. I bet by now you do want to call her." I pick some flowers, three flowers that extend out past the fence of a nearby building. "Here, give her these as soon as you get home."

He accepts them without taking his eyes from me.

"Best of luck to you," I say, remembering his words in the elevator, and I start to walk away.

I pass by the car and reach through the back window to pick up my towel. I cross to the other sidewalk, returning. I wait for a light, the towel draped over my arm the way a waiter would carry it. I look at my feet, my slippers, and I focus on their rhythm; I take in a lot of air and let it out meticulously, aware of its sound and intensity. *This is my way of walking*, I think. *This is my building. This is the code for the front door. This is the button for the elevator that will take me to my floor.* The doors close. When they open, the hallway lights flicker again. Outside my apartment I rewrap my hair in the towel. The door isn't locked. I open it slowly, and everything, everything in the living room and the kitchen, is terrifyingly unchanged. The blanket is tossed at the foot of the sofa, the butts and the mugs are on the coffee table. The furniture, all the pieces of furniture are in their places, storing and supporting all the objects I can remember. And he is still at the table, waiting. He lifts his head from his crossed arms and looks at me. *I went out for a while*, I think. I know it was my turn to talk, but if he asks, that's all I'm going to say.

MORE UNMISSABLE TRANSLATED
FICTION FROM ONEWORLD

A Perfect Crime by A Yi (Chinese)
Translated by Anna Holmwood

Fever Dream by Samanta
Schweblin (Spanish, Argentina)
Translated by Megan McDowell

Frankenstein in Baghdad by
Ahmed Saadawi (Arabic, Iraq)
Translated by Jonathan Wright

Laurus by Eugene Vodolazkin
(Russian)
Translated by Lisa C. Hayden

Little Eyes by Samanta Schweblin
(Spanish, Argentina)
Translated by Megan McDowell

Sweet Bean Paste by Durian
Sukegawa (Japanese)
Translated by Alison Watts

The Hen Who Dreamed She Could Fly
by Sun-mi Hwang (Korean)
Translated by Chi-young Kim

*The Invisible Life of Euridice
Gusmão* by Martha Batalha
(Portuguese, Brazil)
Translated by Eric M. B. Becker

The Meursault Investigation by
Kamel Daoud (French, Algeria)
Translated by John Cullen

The Unit by Ninni Holmqvist
(Swedish)
Translated by Marlaine Delargy

Things We Left Unsaid by Zoya
Pirzad (Persian)
Translated by Franklin Lewis

Three Apples Fell from the Sky
by Narine Abgaryan (Russian,
Armenia)
Translated by Lisa C. Hayden

Umami by Laia Jufresa (Spanish,
Mexico)
Translated by Sophie Hughes

Voices of the Lost by Hoda Barakat
(Arabic, Lebanon)
Translated by Marilyn Booth

This World Does Not Belong to Us
by Natalia García Freire
(Spanish, Ecuador)
Translated by Victor
Meadowcroft